MARIE GOURDON

MORE WILDSIDE CLASSICS

MARIE GOURDON
A ROMANCE OF THE LOWER ST. LAWRENCE

MAUD OGILVY

WILDSIDE PRESS

MARIE GOURDON

This edition published in 2006 by Wildside Press, LLC.
www.wildsidepress.com

INTRODUCTION

This little story is founded on an episode in Canadian history which I found an interesting study, namely, the disbanding of a regiment of Scottish soldiers in the neighborhood of Rimouski and the district about Father Point. Many of these stalwart sons of old Scotia who were thus left adrift strangers in a strange land accepted the situation philosophically, intermarried amongst the French families already in that part of the country, and settled down as farmers in a small way. A visit to that part of the country will show what their industry has effected.

Before having been in the district, I had always thought that the coasts of Lower St. Lawrence were almost incapable of any degree of cultivation, and practically of no agricultural value; but when at Father Point, some three summers ago, I was delighted to see all along the sandy road-sides long ridges of ploughed land, with potatoes, cabbages and beans growing in abundance. Back of these ridges, extending for many miles, are large tracts of most luxuriant pasture land on which browse cattle in very excellent condition.

The manners of the people of this district, who, "far from the madding crowd's ignoble strife," live in Utopian simplicity, are most gentle and courteous, and would put to shame those of the dwellers of many a more civilized spot.

It is very curious to trace the Scottish names of these people, handed down as they have been from generation to generation, though their pronunciation is much altered, and in most instances given a French turn, as, for example, Gourdon for Gordon, Noël for Nowell, and many others. However, in a few cases the names are such as even the most ingenious French tongue finds impossible to alter, and they remain in their original form, for example, Burns, Fraser and McAllister. It is strange to hear these names spoken by people who know

no language but the French, and I was much struck by the
incongruity.

M. O.
Montreal, June, 1890.

CHAPTER I.

"Wae's me for Prince Chairlie."
Old Scotch Song.

It was a dark gloomy night in the year 1745. Huge clouds hung in heavy masses over the sky, ready to discharge their heavy burden at any moment. The thunder echoed and re-echoed with deafening crashes, as if the whole artillery of heaven were arrayed in mighty warfare, and shook even the giant crag on which the castle of Dunmorton was situated.

Fierce indeed was the tempest without, but within the castle raged one still fiercer—that of two strong natures fighting a bitter battle. So loud were their voices raised in altercation that the storm without was scarce heeded.

Dunmorton was a fine old castle of the Norman type, with a large moat surrounding it, and having all the characteristics appertaining to the feudal state. To the rear of the moat, behind the castle, stretched broad lands, on which were scattered many cottages, whose occupants had paid feu-duty to the Lords of Dunmorton for many a generation. To the left of these cottages stretched a large pinewood, with thickly grown underbrush, where, in blissful ignorance of their coming fate, luxuriated golden pheasants and many a fat brace of partridge. That night, the depths of the pine forest were shaken, for the storm was worse than usual even for the east coast of Scotland, where storms are so frequent.

Crossing the drawbridge, and coming to the low Norman arched doorway, one entered at once into the hall. This was a lofty room some twelve feet wide. At one end of it was a broad fireplace, where huge resinous pine logs sent up an odor most grateful to the senses and emitted a pleasant, fitful blaze, lighting up, ever and anon, the faces of The McAllister and his second son Ivan.

On the walls hung huge antlers and heads of deer, the trophies of many a hard day's sport, for they had been a race of sportsmen for generations, these McAllisters, a hardy, strong, self-reliant people, like their own harsh mountain breezes.

The two representatives of the race now quarrelling in the hall were both fine looking men, though of somewhat different types. The McAllister was a tall old man over six feet in height, well and strongly built. His hair was iron-grey, his eyes blue and piercing, his nose rather inclined to the Roman type, his mouth large and determined, and his chin firm, square and somewhat obstinate. His eyebrows were very thick and bushy, thus lending to his face a sinister and rather forbidding expression. He wore a rough home-spun shooting suit, and had folded round his shoulders a tartan of the McAllister plaid, which from time to time he pushed from him with a hasty impatient gesture, as he addressed his son in angry, menacing tones,—

"An' I tell ye, Ivan, though ye be my son, never mair shall I call ye so, if ye join the rabble that young scamp has got together, and never mair shall ye darken the doors of Dunmorton if ye gae wi' him. Noo choose between that young pretender and your ain people."

"Father," said Ivan, "he is not a pretender, of that I am convinced, and you will be soon. He is the descendant of our own King James VI. (whose mother was bonnie Queen Mary), and you paid fealty at Holyrood many years ago to King James. My bonnie Prince Chairlie should by rights be sitting on the throne of Scotland, aye, and of England too, and, by the help of Heaven and our guid Scotch laddies, he will be there ere long."

"Never," sneered The McAllister, scornfully. "I am not afraid of that."

"Well, that is comforting to you at any rate, sir; then why care about my going to join his army, for I am going, nothing can stop me now." And Ivan McAllister's bonnie face glowed with an enthusiasm almost pathetic as he thought of his beloved leader, for whom he would stake all his worldly prospects, aye, and if need be his very life.

"Ivan McAllister," said his father, "I thought ye had mair common sense, though it is rare in lads o' your age. Ye can never imagine that a pack o' young idiots are going to overturn the whole country."

"No, sir, I do not, but a mighty army is to join us from the south; in England Prince Chairlie has many friends, and to-morrow I go to join them. The next day a mighty host will move to the west coast to welcome our future King. And then——"

"Do you know, Ivan, that by your mad folly you seriously endanger the McAllister estates? An' though it is well known at court that I am not a Jacobite, yet I have many enemies who will soon tell the King my son is with the rebels. You endanger, too, your brother Nowell's position at court."

"Well, father, I have promised to go, and a McAllister never breaks his word."

"What! you are determined? You persist in your selfish course of folly? You will go in spite of all I say?"

"Yes, father, I must go, my word is pledged."

The McAllister's ruddy face grew white with anger, he clenched his hands as if he would strike his son and by main force reduce him to obedience, then with a great effort he controlled his anger and said in an ominously calm voice: "Then, Ivan McAl-lister, I tell ye, never mair shall ye set foot in this house, at least, when I am above ground; never mair call yourself son of mine, and may——" raising his right hand solemnly as if invoking supernatural aid.

But here he was interrupted by a gentle voice which said:

"Nay, nay, Nowell, ye shall not curse your son," and a soft hand was laid on his upraised arm.

The McAllister paused and turned towards the speaker, a gentler expression coming over his stern face, for Lady Jean had the greatest influence over her husband, an influence which was always for good.

She was a tall, slightly built woman of some fifty-eight years of age. Her hair was snow-white, contrasting admirably with her clear complexion and dark eyes, and was combed back high above her forehead, and surmounted by a mutch (cap) of finest lace. She was dressed in a gown of pale green silk, which trailed in soft folds behind her and made a rustling noise as she walked.

A most distinguished lady was Jean McAllister, for the blood of the Stuarts ran in her veins.

Her face was beautiful, though not altogether with the beauty of correct features, and certainly not with the beauty of youth, but it had in it that indescribable loveliness, which one sees only in the faces of very good women. It was what might be called a helpful face, and had upon it that reflection of a divine light—all sympathetic natures possess, to some degree.

> "No angel, but a dearer being all dipt in angel instincts, breathing Paradise."

Her voice was of soft and gentle *timbre*, soothing and tranquillizing even at this heated moment, as she turned to her son and said:—

"Oh, me bairn, me bonnie bairn, could ye no' stay wi' us a while longer? It is sair and lonely wi'out ye here, and Prince Chairlie has many mair to fight for him. Can ye not stay wi' us?"

"No, mother dear; much as I should like to be wi' ye all, I fear I cannot. A promise is a promise, you know. *You* have always taught me that. Remember our motto, 'For God and the truth.' You would not wish me to be the first McAllister who broke his word."

"Ah! my dear one," sobbed his mother, now fairly breaking down and weeping piteously, "must ye go, must ye go?"

"Yes, mother dear; but don't distress yourself about me, I shall be all right, and when bonnie Prince Chairlie comes into his own, we shall meet again, and you, my ain bonnie mither, will be one of the first ladies at the court of Holyrood. Now I must go. Father," he said, turning to The McAllister, who was watching the scene in grim silence with folded arms and countenance cold and stern. "Father, do you mean what you said just now? Do you mean to say you will never forgive me if I go to my prince?"

"Yes," the old man thundered out. "Yes, by heaven, I do mean it."

"Then you have driven me for ever from you, and I leave your house tonight. You are hard, unjust, cruel," and, kissing Lady Jean, hastily, without more ado, Ivan left the hall. Then he walked swiftly into the court yard, saddled his favorite horse, and whistling to his collie dog rode off into the dark tempestuous night to face the unknown.

The unknown is always terrible, but at three and twenty the heart is light, care is easily shaken off, and hope springs up eternal. A merciful gift of the good God this, and more especially so in the case of Ivan McAllister, for, poor lad, he was doomed to have many disappointments.

Some weeks after leaving his father's house, he joined the

troops of the young Pretender, Charles Edward; and three days afterwards was fought the battle of Culloden, a battle fraught with such disastrous results to the hopes of many gallant and enthusiastic Scotchmen.

CHAPTER II.

"Oh! Canada, mon pays, terre adorée,
Sol si cher à mes amours"
French Canadian Folk Song

It was a bright August afternoon. The sun was shining down with that intense brilliancy which, I think, is only to be seen in Canada, or in the sunny climes of those countries bordering on the Mediterranean sea. The little village of Rimouski seemed this afternoon all asleep, for the heat made every one drowsy, and the old French Canadian women at their doorsteps were nodding sleepily over their spinning-wheels. Spinning-wheels, improbable as it sounds to nineteenth century ears, are not yet out of date in this part of the country, and many a table-cloth and fine linen sheet, spun by the women of the district, find their way to the shops of Quebec and Montreal. A quaint picturesque little village this; the houses are scattered and at uneven distances from each other. Nearly all of them have large verandahs projecting far out on the roadside, which is covered with uneven planks,—pitfalls in many places to the benighted traveller. There are not many houses of importance here, but there is a fine convent, where the young women of the district are sent to be educated. There is also a school for boys, which adjoins the house of M. le curé. The shops—picture it, ye dwellers in Montreal or Quebec!—are three in number, and are carried on in the co-operative style. Every-thing may be bought in them, from a box of matches or a pound of tobacco, to the fine black silk to serve for a Sunday gown for Madame De la Garde, the lady of the Seigneury.

Then, of course, there is the church, for in what village, how-ever small, in Lower Canada is there not a church? This particular one is not very interesting. It is very large, and has the inevitable tin roof common to most Canadian churches, a glaringly ugly object to behold on a hot afternoon, taking away by its obtrusiveness the restful feeling one naturally associates with a sacred edifice. This on the outside; inside, fortunately, all is different, and more like the Gothic architecture of Northern France than one would imagine from the exterior.

Next comes the railway station, a large ugly building painted a neutral brown. Here everything was very quiet this afternoon, for except at the seasons of the pilgrimages to the church of the Good Saint Anne of Father Point, five miles lower down the line, there is as a rule little traffic going on.

Between Rimouski and Father Point (called by the French Pointe à Père) is a long dusty road, very flat, and, except where the gulf comes in to the coast in frequent little bays, very uninteresting.

There are few houses on this road, and these are far apart.

At the doorstep of one of these cottages—a well-kept, clean and neat little dwelling—sat, this August afternoon, an old woman, spinning busily. She, although some of her neighbors might be, was not asleep. Oh, no! Seldom was Madame McAllister caught napping, save at orthodox hours, between ten p.m. and six a.m. In spite of her seventy-six years, was she hale and hearty, bright and active. She was a brisk little body, and had a most intelligent face. Her eyes were dark and bright with animation, and her coloring was brown and healthy, unlike that of her neighbors of the same age, for, as a rule, French Canadian women of the lower classes lead very hard-working lives, often marrying at sixteen or seventeen, and have scarcely any youth, entering, as they do, on the trials and duties of womanhood before an English girl of the same age has left the schoolroom.

But, as I said before, Madame McAllister was hale and hearty. This circumstance was due most probably to the admixture of Scottish blood in her veins, for her grandfather, Peter Fraser, had been one of the stanchest adherents of the young Pretender. Disappointed in his hopes, he had come out to Quebec to help in the wars against the French, and, after his regiment had been disbanded near Rimouski, he remained in the district. His colonel, a certain Ivan McAllister, persuaded many of his men to remain in that part of the country with him, cherishing the quixotic hope that in this new world he might form a kingdom over which his idol, Prince Chairlie, should reign.

However, after struggling for some years to make a stronghold for his rather erratic chieftain, he at length lost heart and gave up his idea.

Most of his men remained in the district, and intermarried with the French families already settled there.

Poor Colonel McAllister never got over the blow to his hopes. For the sake of the bonnie prince, so unworthy of his true devotion, he had been estranged from his family, and had spent his small fortune in coming to Canada. Here he was, perforce, obliged to remain.

After a while he settled down as a farmer, and managed to make enough to keep body and soul together. Perhaps one of the most sensible things he ever did was to marry Eugenie Laforge, the daughter of the mayor of Rimouski. She was a pretty girl, and had a nice little fortune, for money went further in those days than it does now; and thus the McAllisters were fairly well to do.

Their life for ten years was a happy, uneventful one, most of it spent by the colonel in writing an account of Prince Charlie's adventures. This unfortunate young man, I need hardly remind the reader, had long ago, in the dissipations of various European courts, forgotten that there still existed such a person as Ivan McAllister.

True, the colonel did give certain spare hours to the education of his son, but the Prince was ever first in his mind. One morning,—strangely enough, the anniversary of the battle of Culloden—Ivan McAllister died quietly after a few hours' illness. Even at the last he was true to his idol, for his parting words were not addressed to wife or child, but it seemed that memory, bridging over the gulf of years, brought him back to the old days, and there was something very pathetic in his dying words: "Oh, my Prince, my bonnie Prince, I shall see you soon!"

He was buried, according to a wish he had expressed some years before, in the churchyard of Rimouski, and at the head of his grave was placed a roughly hewn cross, bearing on it this inscription: "Here lies Ivan McAllister, Colonel, of the 200th Regiment of Highlanders, second son of The McAllister of Dunmorton Castle Fife, Scotland. R. I. P."

In his later days Ivan McAllister had, under the influence of the curé of Rimouski, become a devout Roman Catholic.

His son inherited his little savings, and lived on at the farm, situated between Father Point and Rimouski, and the McAllisters continued there from father to son up to the year 1877, when my story opens.

Madame McAllister, sitting at the doorstep this summer afternoon was the widow of a Robert McAllister, who had died two years ago, leaving one son, a promising young man of three-and-twenty. Just now she was waiting for the home-coming of her son Noël, who had been absent on a long fishing expedition to the north shore of the St. Lawrence.

Suddenly the old lady lifted her head, for her quick ear heard the sound of an approaching footstep. She rose hurriedly, as her son drew near, and cried out in her pretty French voice: "Oh, Noël, my son, is that you?—is it indeed you? How long you have been away! and, oh! how I have missed you! Noël, my son, it is good to see you again."

"Yes, my mother, it is I. We landed at Father Point early this morning. We have had such good sport, and very hard work. I am hungry, though, my mother, for the walk up to Rimouski gave me an appetite."

"Yes, my son, you must be. For three days, at this hour I have had a meal prepared for you, and yet you did not come. I was beginning to get anxious, though the Gulf is like glass, and the curé said there were no signs of a storm. Tonight also your supper awaits you, so come in."

The old lady led the way into the house, which was small, but exquisitely neat and well kept. The first apartment, which opened from a tiny hall, served as sitting and dining room. Like most other French Canadian houses, Madame McAllister's was carpeted in all the rooms with a rag carpet of three colors—red, white and blue. This carpeting is extensively woven by the good nuns at Rimouski Convent, and is pretty and effective, besides having the advantage of being cheap.

On the walls of Madame McAllister's sitting room hung the inevitable pictures of the Good St. Anne, the mother of the Blessed Virgin, and of Pope Pius IX. Indeed, it would be difficult to find a house in the district which did not possess one or more of these engravings.

Through a half-opened door could be seen a glimpse of madame's bedroom—a dainty interior. The wooden floor was snowy white, with here and there a bright-colored mat spread on it; the brown roughly-hewn bedstead was covered with a quilt of palest pink and blue patchwork, the patient result of the old lady's years of industrious toil.

Madame McAllister busied herself getting supper ready, all the while talking to her son.

"Well, Noël, my son, what did you get this time? I trust a great quantity."

"Yes, my mother, we did very well. The first day we captured a fine porpoise, and after that six large seals."

"Ah! that was good," replied madame.

Both mother and son spoke French in the Lower Canadian *patois*, rather puzzling to English ears trained to understand only Parisian French. For, not only is the pronunciation different, but several Scotch words are used by the inhabitants of this district, and one puzzles hopelessly over their derivation, until remembering the origin of the people.

"Where did you leave your boat?" questioned madame.

"At Father Point light-house with Jean Gourdon. He is to drive up with the pilot tomorrow, and by that time will have skinned the seals."

"Surely the steamer is late this week?"

"Yes, but she will pass Father Point early tomorrow morning; she was telegraphed from Matane, where there has been a dense fog."

"I am glad, Noël, you had such good luck this time."

"Yes, the porpoise will keep us in oil all winter, and as for the seal-skins, I can sell them at Quebec for a good round price. So far so good. But this is the first stroke of luck this year. It has been a poor season. Have you any news, my mother?"

"No, nothing much, my son. There is to be a great pilgrimage to the shrine of the Good St. Anne next week. Hundreds of lame, blind and sick folk are coming from all parts of the country—from Quebec, and even from Gaspé. Oh, my son, it is wonderful what the Good St. Anne does for her children."

"Yes, yes," said Noël, impatiently, "but I want to hear the news of the people here. How is Marie Gourdon?"

"Marie Gourdon? Oh! much as usual—always singing or playing the organ at the church, and M. Bois-le-Duc encourages her. I call it nonsense myself," and the old lady shrugged her shoulders deprecatingly.

"But, my mother, she sings like an angel."

"Yes, yes, Noël; so Eugène Lacroix says too."

"Eugène Lacroix!" said Noël, starting; "I thought he was in Montreal."

"He has been here for the last week. He came down for a holiday, and is always with Marie Gourdon."

"Yes, yes, they are old friends. I do not care much for Eugène Lacroix. He seems to me a dreamy, impractical sort of person, and only thinks of his books and those absurd pictures he is always making."

"You think them absurd?" replied madame.

"M. Bois-le-Duc told me he had great talent. You know that, for a time the curé sent him to Laval at his own expense, and now talks of sending him to Paris."

"To Paris! and for what purpose?"

"Oh! the curé thinks he will make a great painter. He is always painting during his holidays. I'm sure I can't see the good of it."

"Well, my mother, M. Bois-le-Duc is a very clever man, and whatever he does is good, but I, for one, have no very high opinion of Eugène Lacroix."

While this conversation had been going on, Noël McAllister did ample justice to the good fare his mother set before him. Madame McAllister was nothing if not practical, and cooking was one of her strong points. Her *bouillon*, a sort of hotch-potch, was so good that a hungry Esau might well have bartered his birthright for it. Her pancakes and *galettes* were marvels of culinary skill.

Noël, having appeased his appetite, sharpened by the salt sea breezes, and after enjoying a pipe, said, "Now, my mother, I think I shall go out for a walk and hear the news. I shall not be late."

"Very well, my son. Come back soon," said the old lady, and, as she heard the door close on Noël, she smiled grimly to herself and muttered,

"The news, eh? The news! That is to say in plain words, Marie Gourdon."

CHAPTER III.

"Il y a longtemps qui je t'aime,
Jamais je ne t'oublierai."
                              French Canadian Song.

It is a beautiful evening. The tide is rushing in over the crisp yellow sands of the beach at Father Point. The sun is setting slowly, as if loath to leave this part of the world, and, as he departs, touches with his rays the gold and crimson tops of the maple and sumach trees, which border the road leading into the churchyard of the Good St. Anne.

The clouds are scudding over the sky in great masses of copper color and gold, parting every here and there, and showing glimpses of clear translucent blue beyond.

And how quickly the whole panorama changes as the sun sinks to his bed in the sea. Anon everything was golden and amethystine, like a foreshadowing of the splendor of the New Jerusalem. A moment later and all is a deep vivid crimson, flooding the scene with its rich radiance and casting into shade even the tints of yon tall sumach tree in the prime of its early autumn coloring. The old grey slate boulders on the beach are illumined by it, and stand out in prominence from the yellow sands.

All is still tonight, save for the beating of the waves against the rocks, or ever and anon the sound of a gun fired from the distant light-house.

The light-house of Father Point stands out clear and distinct on a long neck of rocky land running into the St. Lawrence.

All is still. But hark! A song comes faintly, carried on the evening breeze, and presently it grows clearer, louder, more distinct.

The words now can be heard plainly. They are those of that old French Canadian song so familiar to all dwellers in the Province of Quebec:

"A la claire fontaine,
M'en allant promener,
J'ai trouvé l'eau si belle
Que je me suis baigné.
Il y a longtemps que je t'aime
Jamais je ne t'oublierai."

The voice was tuneful, strong, and full and clear, though lacking in cultivation. It was that of a girl, who was sitting under the shadow of a large boulder on the beach. She seemed about eighteen, though, in the uncertain wavering light of the sunset, it was impossible to distinguish her features clearly.

Her gown was of simple pink cotton, and on her head she wore a large peaked straw hat, which gave her a quaint old-world appearance.

Her brown hair had escaped from beneath this large head-gear, and blew about in pretty, untidy curls round her neck and shoulders. In her hand was a roll of music, which she had just brought from the church, where she had been practising for the morrow's mass.

The girl was Marie Gourdon, only daughter of old Jean Baptiste Gourdon, fisherman of Father Point. As far as the educational advantages of Father Point and Rimouski could take her Marie had gone, but that was not saying much. Her father was fairly well-to-do for that part of the world, and had sent her, at an early age, to the convent of Rimouski. There she was brought up under the careful training of Mother Annette, the superioress, and received enough musical instruction to enable her to act as organist at the Father Point church, and to direct the choir at Grand Mass.

Marie Gourdon was rather a lonely girl, although she had more outside interests than many of her age. She had few companions, for most of the young girls of the district obtained situations in Quebec, or some of the large towns, finding the dullness of Father Point insupportable. Her father and brother had this summer been on long fishing expeditions, one taking them even so far as the Island of Anticosti, so that Marie was left much to her own devices. Noël McAllister, it is true, was often here, but neither his mother nor M. Bois-le-Duc seemed to like to see him in Marie Gourdon's society.

This evening she had been thinking over these things after choir-practice. Lately she had found time pass very slowly. Her father and brother had come home early in the evening, but went off directly after supper to skin the seals, and she would see no more of them that night. In all probability in a few days they would go on another expedition.

A quick footstep crunching the sand and a voice saying, "Good evening, Marie," made the girl turn round to see Noël McAllister standing beside her.

She sprang to her feet and exclaimed, with a certain glad ring in her voice:

"Oh! Noël, is that you? I am so pleased you are back."

"Yes, Marie, it is I, not my ghost, though you look as if you had seen one. And are you pleased to see me?"

"Of course I am. I think you need scarcely ask that question."

"And what have you been doing, my dear one, since I have been away?"

"Oh! Noël, the time has seemed so long, so wearisome. There has been no one here to speak to, except for a week or two when Eugène Lacroix came home for his holidays. I used to watch him paint, and he talked to me about his work at Laval."

"Marie, I don't like Eugène Lacroix. He is stupid, conceited, impractical."

"Indeed, I think you are mistaken. M. Bois-le-Duc calls him a genius. Eugène, too, is a most interesting companion, and he has told me many tales of countries far beyond here."

"Well, he may be a genius, though I for my part cannot see it. And you, my dear one, do you long to see those countries beyond the sea? I know I do. I am tired of this life, this continual struggle for a bare existence. The same thing day after day, year after year; nothing new happens. Why did M. Bois-le-Duc teach me of an outer world beyond the bleak Gulf of St. Lawrence? Why did he teach me to read Virgil and Plato? He did it for the best, no doubt; but I think he did wrong. He has stirred up within me a restless evil spirit of discontent. Oh! Marie, to think I am doomed to be a fisherman here all my life. It is hard."

"Yes, Noël, it is hard. It has always seemed to me that you with your talents, your learning, are thrown away here. But why not go to Quebec or Montreal? You would have a wider sphere there."

"I would go tomorrow, Marie, if it were not for one thing."

"What is that, Noël?"

"Marie, do you not know?"

"I suppose your reason is that you do not wish to leave your mother," said the girl hesitatingly.

"No, Marie, that is not the reason. My mother would let me go tomorrow, if I wished."

"Then I cannot understand why you stay. You would do much better in Quebec, you with your ability."

"You cannot understand, Marie? You do not know that it is because of *you*, and you alone, that I stay on in this place, smothering all my ambitions, my hopes of advancement. No, Marie, you say you do not understand. If you spoke more truly you would say you did not care where I went."

"Noël," said the girl gently, and looking distressed, "you know, my dear one, that I do care very much, and I cannot think why you speak to me in that bitter way."

"Marie, do you care? You have seemed lately so indifferent to my plans, and it has made me angry, for, my darling, you must have seen that my love for you is deep, strong, mighty, like the flow of yonder great river. Aye, it is stronger, greater, more unchangeable."

A glad light came into the girl's pale face, but she did not speak, and Noël went on:

"It is not as if my love for you were a thing of yesterday, for I can never remember the time when you were not first in my thoughts. Yes, Marie—

> '*Il y a longtemps que je t'aime,*
> *Jamais je ne t'oublierai.*' "

"What, Noël, never? That is a long, long time. Are you sure, Noël?"

"Am I sure, Marie? Is yonder great rock, on which countless tides have beaten, sure? Is the mighty Gulf sure of its ebb and flow? Is anything sure in this world, Marie?"

The girl did not answer, and he went on:

"Tell me, Marie, do you care for me or do you not?"

Marie hesitated, and Noël impatiently gathered up some loose pebbles and threw them into the water, walking hurriedly up and down the beach.

"Marie, you must answer me tonight; I must come to a decision."

The girl rose slowly from her seat, and, coming towards Noël, put both her hands in his, and lifting up her great brown eyes, lighted with happiness and perfect trust, said deliberately,—

> "'Il y a longtemps que je t'aime,
> Jamais je ne t'oublierai.'"

CHAPTER IV.

"Red o'er the forest peers the setting sun,
The line of yellow light dies fast away."

Keble.

"Well, I'm afraid, Webster, it's a thankless task. There are plenty of Scotch names about here, but not the one we want. I'm heartily tired of going about from churchyard to churchyard, poking around like ghouls or medical students. We've been to all the graves in the neighborhood, and, interesting as such a pursuit may be to an antiquary like yourself, I find it very slow. I'm one of those sensible people who believe in living in the present, and letting the dead past bury its dead, as the poet says."

"Are you, indeed?" retorted his companion drily. "Too lazy, I suppose, to do anything else."

"Well, that may be the case; but this I know, that I'm going to cable Lady McAllister tomorrow, and tell her that I'm going back. You may stay here if you like, as you appear to find the country so charming."

"It is very kind, indeed, of you to give me your permission," replied the other. "But, my gay and festive friend, I doubt very much whether Lady McAllister will allow you to return. You know, as well as I, how decided she is. When she has once got an idea into her head, it is hard to get it out."

"But, my dear sir," said the younger man, "it is such an utterly ridiculous idea that she has got into her head now."

"Not quite so ridiculous as you think. It is a well-known fact that, about the year 1754, Ivan McAllister, with a regiment of Scottish soldiers, did embark for Canada, and landed at Quebec. It is just as well known that a Scottish regiment was disbanded near Rimouski a few years later, and we have every reason to believe, from our correspondence with the Quebec Government, that Ivan McAllister settled in this district."

"I grant you all that, but he is dead long ago."

"Yes, but in all probability he has descendants living. If not, of course the McAllister male line is extinct, and Lady McAllister's hopes will receive a terrible blow."

"Poor Lady McAllister! she seems to have taken the thing very much to heart. I hope she won't be disappointed, but I wish I hadn't come on this wild-goose chase."

"You have come," said the elder, "so you had better make the best of it."

"Well, a precious lucky fellow this McAllister will be, if he exists. Why, Dunmorton Castle with its woods must be worth half a million sterling."

"Umph!" said the old man. "There is a condition."

"Yes, yes, but not a very dreadful one. Still, I'm not sure that I'd like to marry Lady Janet myself."

"My young friend, your speculation on the subject is idle, for you will never get the chance."

"Well, it doesn't matter," said his young friend philosophically, and with a sentimental air, "my heart is another's."

"Ah, indeed! And who may the un—" (he had nearly said unfortunate, but corrected himself in time) "fortunate damsel be?"

"Miss Sally Perkins. Yes, she is the girl of my choice. Oh! that I had never crossed the briny ocean, so far away from Clapham and my Sally. The Sunday I broke the news of my departure to her I shall never forget. It was at tea; we were eating shrimps and brown bread and butter. She had just poured out tea, and had eaten only two shrimps, when I told her I was going across the broad Atlantic. She could eat no more shrimps that day. She was overcome."

"Poor Miss Perkins!" said his companion. "Sure devotion could no further go. She must be very fond of you."

"She is; and I must go back to England."

"You have come, and now I advise you to wait till I return. And, let me tell you that cabling is very expensive just now. You will only waste your money for nothing, and besides will be snubbed for your pains by Lady McAllister."

The speaker who gave this sage advice was a little old man, with a wizened face like parchment. His keen blue eyes had a shrewd twinkle in them, and altogether he gave one the impression that he could see further into a stone wall than most people. He was the confidential lawyer and intimate friend of Lady McAllister, of Dunmorton Castle in Fife, and had served the family for more than forty years.

His companion was a young Londoner, somewhat of the Cockney stamp, by name Thomas Brown, a youth chiefly celebrated for his immense estimation of his own capabilities.

The two men had arrived a week before by one of the mail steamers, and had, in accordance with Lady McAllister's commands, visited nearly every churchyard in the district to discover the name of McAllister.

Hitherto this had been a thankless task. Now, dispirited and fatigued, they were leaning upon the rough wooden fence which divided the burying ground of Father Point church from the road. This church, dedicated to the Good St. Anne, had been built by the pious efforts of pilots on the ships plying the River St. Lawrence and the Gulf. It was intended to be a thankful recognition to their patron saint for their deliverance from the perils of the deep.

And the church had become a noted place for pilgrimages. Indeed, it was said that miraculous cures were effected by the agency of a sacred relic of St. Anne, and many a sufferer was brought here in the hope that, by performing his devotions at the shrine of St. Anne, he would be cured of his maladies.

There was something very pathetic about the lonely little churchyard of Father Point, with its borders of overgrown raspberry bushes straggling in untidy clusters round the graves. At one end of the ground were five graves, marked each by plain wooden crosses, painted a dull black, with the Christian names in white of those who slept beneath. These rough crosses marked the resting-places of the good nuns, who had spent their lives working in this part of the country. All that is left to serve as remembrance of their struggles, their trials, their brief glimpses of happiness, are these wooden crosses, from which the rain of a few autumn days effaced even the names of those who labored so long and faithfully.

This evening everything is very calm and still, and the peace of nature is only disturbed by the tinkling of the bells on the necks of the cattle as they are driven home by the French Canadian cowherds. A silence seems to have settled over the whole face of nature. Presently, however, from the open windows of the church comes a song, faint at first, but swelling louder and stronger, on the evening breeze:

> "*Maria, Maria, ora pro nobis,*
> *Ora, ora pro nobis, Sancta Maria.*"

It is the evening hymn of the curé and his acolytes pealing out on the still evening air. Higher and higher one treble voice goes like the cry of a soul in agonized entreaty:

> "*Maria, Maria, Sancta Maria,*
> *Ora, ora pro nobis.*"

Then it dies away, and all is still except the ever-present swish! swish! of the rising tide against the great boulders on the beach.

"Oh! I say, Webster," said young Brown, in his mincing, affected tone, "why not, after they have finished in there," he pointed to the church, "go in and ask the priest whether he knows anything of these people? He ought to know them if anyone does. Good idea, eh?"

"Yes," said the old lawyer, turning round suddenly and looking rather annoyed, for in spite of his hard crust of Scotch dryness, his young clerk's voice has jarred on him at this moment. He had been deeply moved by the beauty of the scene, and the sweet tones coming from the church had stirred within him long-forgotten memories.

"Yes, for once you have hit on a bright idea, and we will act on it. Let us go in and see the priest. And, my young friend, remember that most of these priests are gentlemen, so mind your manners."

"I expect that house next the church is his," replied young Brown. "We can walk slowly on, and, in the meantime, the priest will come from his devotions."

CHAPTER V.

"A parish priest was of the pilgrim train;
An awful reverend and religious man.
His eyes diffused a venerable grace,
And charity itself was in his face.
Rich was his soul, though his attire was poor
(As God hath clothed his own ambassador),
For such, on earth, his bless'd Redeemer bore."

Dryden.

Réné Bois-le-Duc, curé of Father Point, had just come home, and was preparing to take his ease after a hard day's toil, anticipating the arrival of the pilgrims, who were about to visit the church of the Good St. Anne.

The curé was a man of some sixty years of age, though looking older, for his had been a hard and toilsome life. Though secluded from the busy world, he had had heavy responsibilities forced upon him, and there was no one of his own class and education in these parts to cheer and sympathize with him in his rare moments of leisure.

Belonging to one of the oldest families in Brittany, Réné Bois-le-Duc had, in spite of the strong attractions of worldly society, early conceived a high ideal of what life ought to be.

This ideal was fostered by the influence of his instructors at college. His enthusiastic temperament and ascetic leanings led him to think seriously of entering holy orders when quite young, but this idea met with strong opposition from his parents; so, for a time, he abandoned it.

In Paris for one short winter with his elder brother Octave, he was much sought after for his rare musical talents, as well as his personal attractiveness, which charmed all with whom he came in contact. Madame la Marquise was proud of both her sons, but Réné she idolized, and he returned her affection with a devotion rare even in the best of children.

Like a sudden clap of thunder, there came on the gay world of Paris one spring morning the news that Réné Bois-le-Duc had joined the great Dominican order, and had been hurriedly sent off at a moment's notice on a mission to America. At first it could not be believed possible; but at length, after a year when he did not return, the fact could not be doubted. But what was the reason for this sudden step? Why had he not told his friends? Why did he leave in this way? There was a mystery about it, and his former friends were not slow in inventing evil reports about the absent one. Octave Bois-le-Duc never mentioned his brother, nor was the mystery ever cleared up.

All this, of course, happened many years before my story opens; and though at first Réné Bois-le-Duc found his new life hard, exiled as he was from all his former associates, he had never returned to France. At times he had been sorely tempted to do so, but he knew that none could replace him in his work at Father Point, and he had grown to love his people—to be, indeed, a father unto them, mindful both of their spiritual and temporal well-being.

Nor can it be said that his talents were entirely thrown away, for from time to time some highly polished poem or literary critique would find its way from the lonely little house on the banks of the St. Lawrence to a standard French magazine; and old schoolmates of the curé would shrug their shoulders and say, "Oh, here is a capital thing by Réné Bois-le-Duc. I thought he was dead and buried long ago."

And he was, indeed, so far as men of his own standing and education were concerned. Except for an annual visit from his bishop, and occasionally one from a pilot or sea captain, M. Bois le-Duc seldom heard news of the outer world. On the whole, his life was not an unhappy one, and certainly not idle. Most of the hours not spent in parish work were occupied in perfecting the education of several of the young men in whom he was interested. With Noël McAllister he took special pains. Whether the results were satisfactory in this particular case may be doubted; still he did what he considered best, and left the issue to Providence.

In Marie Gourdon, too, he took a great interest. Her mother had died when she was scarcely six months old. Her father had never troubled his dull head about her; and, after she left the convent at Rimouski, she led a very lonely life for so young a girl.

There was much to interest even such a cultivated man as M. Bois-le-Duc in Marie Gourdon. She had inherited from her mother a remarkable talent for music, such as many of the French Canadians have strongly developed. Her soprano voice was powerful, clear and flexible, and her ear was very correct. The good curé judged that, if given proper training, and the advantages Paris alone could afford, the little Canadian girl might become an artist of the first rank. But how send her to Paris? The thing seemed impossible. Where was the money to come from? True, M. le curé had been well paid for his last review in the Catholic Journal, but he had exhausted this money in sending Eugène Lacroix, another *protégé*, to Laval for a twelvemonth. Alas now his treasury was empty; his cupboard was bare!

This evening he was thinking all these matters over, when suddenly he was roused from his meditations by the voice of Julie, his old housekeeper, calling out:

"M. le curé, there is a gentleman asking for you at the door."

"For me, Julie, at this hour? Who is he?"

"Not a Frenchman, that is very certain, monsieur; I should think not, indeed; his accent is execrable;" and the good woman lifted her hands with a gesture of despair.

"Could you not understand what he wanted?" asked the priest.

"No, monsieur; the only word I could make out was '*la cooré*,' so I thought that might mean you."

"Well, well," said M. Bois-le-Duc, laughing, "the best thing is for me to see him myself."

He went out into the tiny dark passage where Mr. Webster and his clerk were standing.

"Good-evening," he said, in his polished courtly manner. "I must apologize for having kept you waiting so long. Pray come into my study. I fear Julie was somewhat brusque and rude to you. She is a good soul, though. Please be seated, gentlemen."

"M. *la cooré*," said Webster, struggling hard with his one French word, and breaking down lamentably.

"I can speak English," said the priest, "if that will help you."

"Oh, yes," replied Webster, drawing a deep sigh of relief; "thank Heaven for that."

M. le curé smiled benignly.

"Well, sir," went on the lawyer, "I've come to ask you whether you knew a family called McAllister, supposed to be living in these parts."

"McAllister! Why, of course I do. I have known them for years."

"Oh, my good sir, you have relieved my mind of a heavy burden. For the last three weeks my clerk and I have been searching every churchyard round about here for the name, and have hitherto failed to find it. Tonight the idea entered my head that you might know."

"My head, if you please," murmured young Brown *sotto voce*.

"I shall be most happy to be of any service to you," said M. Bois-le-Duc. "Madame McAllister, with her son Noël, lives about three miles down the road. You cannot mistake the cottage. It is a plain white one with a red-tiled roof—the only red-roofed cottage on the road."

"Thank you very much, sir," said Webster.

"You will like Noël McAllister," went on the curé; "he is a fine manly young fellow, and was my pupil for many years, so I know him well."

"I am infinitely obliged to you, sir," said Webster, gratefully. "I suppose we may call at the cottage the first thing in the morning. The only house on the road with a red-tiled roof you said? Thanks. We shall not detain you longer. Good-evening, sir, good-evening."

And Webster, having obtained the desired information, marched off with his clerk, leaving the curé in wondering perplexity as to his relations with the McAllisters.

CHAPTER VI.

"The love of money is the root of all evil."

"Yes, Mr. McAllister, there is no choice. The estates are so left by the old lord that unless you marry your cousin you can have no part of them. An empty title you will have, to be sure; much good that is to anyone nowadays! In case of your refusing the conditions imposed upon you by the late lord's will, which Lady McAllister is determined to see faithfully carried out, my advice to you is to stay here and remain a fisherman all your life. A pleasant prospect that for a young fellow of your talents."

"I must marry my cousin?" questioned Noël.

"Yes, that is imperative."

"What is she like?"

"Oh, she is like herself, no one else I ever saw. I'm not good at descriptions, especially of ladies. She has yellow hair, I can tell you that."

"Yellow hair—yes, yes; but her disposition, her character? Is she amiable?"

"Well, I don't think that amiable is quite the word to apply to Lady Margaret. She is self-reliant, sensible, a thorough woman of business, and the very one to help you on in the world."

"Oh, indeed; but if I ever possess Dunmorton I shall be helped on enough."

"What! have you no wish for more? Would you not like to go into Parliament to make a name for yourself? Your cousin could help you in that. They say she used to write all her father's speeches, and very good speeches they were."

"And Marie Gourdon?" said Noël slowly. "What of her? How can I leave her?"

"Oh, nonsense!" said the little lawyer impatiently; "really I wonder at a man of your sense hesitating in such a matter. This

Marie will get over it; all girls do. It's only a matter of time. She'll forget all about you in a month."

Noël's thoughts went back to the scene on the beach two evenings ago, and he did not consider it at all probable that Marie Gourdon would ever forget him. At any rate, he did not care to entertain the possibility.

"Yes," went on Webster, "I don't see that you can have any hesitation. Here you are, at the opening of your life, offered one of the finest chances I ever heard of, hesitating because of a little French girl. Umph! I've no patience with you, but, young man, you've got to decide before tomorrow's mail goes out. I must write to Lady McAllister. Good-bye I'm going for a walk to the lighthouse. The keeper is a most interesting man, and a great mathematician. Good-bye. I hope next time I see you you'll have come to your senses."

And Webster walked off, evidently imagining that there could be no hesitation about the matter of the inheritance.

The whole of that day was a miserable failure to Noël McAllister. He had one of those natures which hate making a decision. He was restless, and could settle down to nothing, and walked up and down his mother's little verandah like a caged animal. He could not bear the thought of giving up Marie, yet, on the other hand, he could not bear the thought of giving up his inheritance. It was too tempting. To leave forever the monotony of a life at Father Point, to plunge all at once into luxury and riches, that was a dazzling prospect, with only Marie Gourdon on the other side to counter-balance these attractions. And she had been so slow in telling him she cared for him that even now he half doubted whether she really did, in spite of the truthfulness in her great brown eyes, when she repeated the refrain of that old French song. And the lawyer had said she would forget in a month, like all other girls, and she was not different from other girls. Yes, it was a difficult question to decide, there was no doubt about that. He despised himself for thinking of giving up Marie, the mere thought horrified him, and yet—Dunmorton, ease, riches, luxury!

To give all these up without a struggle would have been difficult, even to a more heroic nature than Noël McAllister's.

There was not long, however, for him to decide the question, and as evening came on, and he thought that by next morning the die must be cast one way or the other, his head ached with the effort of anxious thought. Fresh air he felt he must have, so he went out from the cottage, and walked hurriedly down the road.

The moon was shining cold and clear, showing distinctly the delicate tracery of each branch and leaf overhanging the pathway. The cold, clear light threw into strong relief each giant maple tree darkly looming against the silvery evening sky.

McAllister walked hurriedly on, deeply thinking, for about a quarter of a mile. His head was bent, and he saw nothing, so absorbed was he in his own meditations. Presently, however, a figure crossed his path. He started, and looked up to see a girl in a red cloak standing in the pathway. She stopped before him. It was Marie Gourdon, the last person in the world he wished to meet just then.

"Marie, my dear one," he said, "what are you doing out so far alone, and at this hour too? Come; let me take you home."

"Noël, I came to see you. I hoped to have met you. I have something important to say to you."

"Indeed, Marie, what can it be? You should have sent for me. You cannot talk to me here. Let me take you home, and then you can tell me."

"No, no," said Marie persistently. "Jean and my father are in the house, and I wish to speak to you alone, and what I am going to tell you I must say tonight."

"What is this tremendous secret?"

She did not answer the question but said abruptly:

"M. Bois-le-Duc tells me you are going away."

"Going away? Um—um—I don't know," Noël replied hesitatingly. "I think not. No no, M. Bois-le-Duc makes a great mistake."

"You are not going away?" said the girl, a glad light coming into her eyes. "What, Noël you have not come into this fortune?"

"Oh! yes, there is no doubt about that; but there are conditions, and I can't accept them."

"What are the conditions?"

"One is that I shall have to leave you, to give you up."

"Noël, there would be no need of that."

"Why, what do you mean, Marie?"

"I give *you* up," said Marie proudly. "I could never stand in your way of advancement."

"Marie, did you not say to me most solemnly only the other night:

*'Il y a longtemps que je t'aime,
Jamais je ne t'oublierai.'*"

"What has that to do with it, Noël? That does not alter the case. It is just because of that I will not let you stay here. You may think it an easy thing to decide now, but in after years you would regret remaining here. With your gifts, your ambition, you would be thrown away. No, Noël, *I* bid you go. You must not stay. Good-bye, dear one, for the last time. You must tell them tomorrow that you will go."

"It is impossible," said Noël, in an angry tone. "You can never have cared for me to give me up in a moment like this."

"You know that is not true, Noël. I can see into the future, and it is just because I do care so much for you that I do not wish you to waste your life here." She spoke with an effort, and as if she were repeating a lesson learned beforehand.

"No, that is not it," said Noël; "I am perfectly sure you never cared for me or you could not give me up like this in a moment."

The girl did not answer for a time, for she was deeply wounded at his want of understanding, his non-comprehension of her most unselfish motives. Presently she turned to him, and said in a hurried tone, for she could scarcely control herself just then, "Noël, believe me it is for the best. Good-bye."

Before he had time to answer she had walked swiftly away, and was hid from his sight by the turn of the road. All had happened so quickly, the momentous decision had been made so entirely without effort on his part, that his breath was fairly taken away. But, beneath all his surprise and wounded pride was a feeling of relief scarce acknowledged to himself, though his first exclamation was one of distressed self-love, as he exclaimed angrily, "She has no feeling; she does not care."

Ah! M. Bois-le-Duc, your training of Noël McAllister was at fault somewhere. You grounded him thoroughly in Latin and the classics, but you taught him little of the study of human character, that most profoundly interesting of all studies. Had your teaching been different, Noël McAllister might have had a different estimation of the depths of a nature like Marie Gourdon's, of a woman's true unselfish devotion. He might have made an effort to keep what he had already won—which was above all price. Had your teaching not failed in this one essential point, Noël McAllister's life and career would have been far different. Well for him had it been so!

CHAPTER VII.

"O world! thy slippery turns! Friends, now fast sworn in love
inseparable, shall within this hour break out to bitterest enmity."
Coriolanus, Act iv., Scene iv.

It was two months later, a chilly October afternoon.

The glory of the maple and the sumach had departed, and a
dingy russet brown had succeeded the more brilliant tints of early
autumn. The tide was high, and the waves dashed angrily against
the long pier at Rimouski.

On this pier were gathered six persons, awaiting the arrival
from Quebec of the outward-bound steamer. They were Madame
McAllister and her son Noël, Marie Gourdon, Pierre, her father,
Jean, her brother, and M. Bois-le-Duc. What was the matter with
M. le curé this afternoon? He looked anxious and care-worn, and
scarcely spoke to anyone. Marie, on the contrary, was very bright,
and tried to keep up Madame McAllister's spirits, which were at
the lowest ebb.

On the whole, there was not much talking done, for a cloud
seemed to hang over the whole party.

Presently, some miles out on the gulf, at first like a tiny black
speck, appeared the steamer. Nearer and nearer it came, growing
larger and larger as it approached. The dark waters heaved up in
huge waves as her bow pierced their depths. The foam dashed
high, as if in angry protest at the intruder. And Madame McAllister, glancing at the ship, said in her quaint, pathetic way: "Ah!
Noël, my son, here is the ship like some huge monster come to
swallow you up. I cannot let you go. Oh! my son, my son!"

At length the steamer "Peruvian"—for Lady McAllister desired that Noël should travel in every way befitting her heir—
reached the pier. Ropes were thrown out and caught by the fish-
ermen.

The mails, in great leather bags, were thrown on board, and shouts were heard of "All passengers aboard!"

During all this bustle Noël McAllister stepped aside, and said to M. Bois-le-Duc, in a hurried, anxious tone:

"And now, my father, are you not going to give me your blessing?"

M. Bois-le-Duc, strangely enough, had made no advance towards his favorite pupil; in fact, during the whole of the last month had seemed to avoid him. Now, when thus directly questioned, he answered:

"Yes, Noël, I wish you all happiness in your new life, and hope you will have a safe and pleasant voyage."

"And is that all you have to say to me, my father?"

The curé did not reply, but pointed to Madame McAllister, who was gazing at her son with eager, wistful eyes, jealously counting every moment of absence from her side. He obeyed the curé's unspoken command, and returned to his mother, conscience-stricken at the silent rebuke of this his best and most valued friend.

No change of plan was possible now. The die was cast for good or evil. Weakness had triumphed over strength. Blame him—he was worthy of blame; but, pausing for a moment, may it not be said that nine men out of ten would have decided as did Noël McAllister?

"Oh! my mother, you know I shall write every week. Do not distress yourself. Marie, good-bye. Remember always it was you who bade me go. Good-bye, Monsieur Gourdon. Good-bye, Jean."

He was off at last, and the steamer moved out from the pier. How bitter these partings are and how hard to bear, but the thought crossed M. Bois-le-Duc's mind just then that there were worse things than partings.

"Take me home," said Madame McAllister. "I cannot stay here watching my boy disappear."

She was terribly distressed, and the curé and Jean Gourdon led her home. No one seemed to think of Marie. She had disappeared behind a huge pile of lumber, and had sat down to rest on a great log. There she sat for she knew not how long; she seemed unconscious, oblivious of all, save that tiny black speck which was sinking lower and lower on the horizon. Finally it disappeared down the great waste of interminable ocean.

The sun set, and the air grew chill; the tide rose high; the curlews hovered round with their weird cries; the Angelus from the church came wafted across the waters, faint and sweet in its distant music, and the laborers in the fields paused a moment in their tasks to do homage to the Holy Maiden in murmured prayers. But Marie Gourdon heard none of these sounds, felt not the cold of the evening air. Her senses were benumbed, and she was only conscious of a dull, aching pain.

Two hours passed, and during these two hours Marie fought out her battle with herself. When M. le curé missed her, he went to look for her at her father's house, and not finding her there, the idea occurred to him that she might be still on the pier. Returning, he found her. Laying a gentle hand on her down-bent head, he said:

"My child, come home with me. You must not give way like this, such grief is wrong, and—he is not worthy of it."

"Oh! my father," said Marie, lifting a wan, white face to his, "life is indeed hard."

"Yes," said the curé, raising his hat reverently, and looking out towards the cold, unfathomable waters of the great Gulf. "And, my child, there is only One who can help us on that rough path."

CHAPTER VIII

TEN YEARS AFTER.

"Oh! wouldst thou set thy rank before thyself?
Wouldst thou be honored for thyself or that?
Rank that excels the wearer, doth degrade,
Riches impoverish that divide respect."

Sheridan Knowles

The morning-room at Glen McAllister was an ideal room of its kind, in a rather plain and severe style. The floor was covered with dainty blue and white straw matting, and huge rugs of musk-ox skin, from the wilds of the great North-West of Canada, were scattered here and there about the room. At a large desk, looking as if it might belong to a man with an immense business connection, sat Lady Margaret McAllister. She was adding accounts with a methodical accuracy and speed even a bank clerk could not hope to excel. She was a woman of about forty, though looking younger, her hair being of that tawny shade of yellow that rarely turns grey, and her complexion bright and fresh, bearing witness to a healthy outdoor life.

That morning she was very busy counting up the week's expenses, and trying to explain to her husband that the conduct of their bailiff was most reprehensible. Lady Margaret always used long words in preference to short ones, which might express exactly the same meaning. This was one of her peculiarities.

"Three months' rent for the Mackay's farm is due, Noël. I really think you might bestir yourself a little to look after the estate. Jones is the most execrable manager I ever knew. Here you are, with nothing to do all day except smoke or shoot, letting things go to rack and ruin. We shall be in the poor-house soon. Umph! I've no patience with you."

"No, my dear, you never had, and each year you have less. I

am, indeed, a sore trial to you," replied her husband, smiling placidly.

"You are, there can be no question about that," said Lady Margaret, bitterly.

Noël took his cigar out of his mouth, looked at her calmly for a moment, and said:

"Then why——"

"Why—Yes, I know what you are going to say, you have said it so frequently—why did I marry you?" she interrupted.

"You have guessed rightly, my dear; that was just what I was about to remark."

"I married you because I could not help myself."

"Oh, yes, you could. You might have refused, and I would have gone back to Canada—would gladly have done so."

"No, Noël," said his wife, rising and standing before him, a rather terrifying figure; "be at least truthful. You would not have given up the estate even though it was burdened with an incubus like me."

"Well, well, my dear," said Noël, yawning aggravatingly, "all that is over. As your poet says, 'Let the dead past bury its dead.'"

"Inexact in small things as well as great," said Lady Margaret, who had returned to her accounts. "Your poet, you mean, for your quotation is from Longfellow, and he lived nearer your country than mine."

"Oh! I never remember these fellows' names. I take it for granted you are right. You always are, my dear. But let us return to prose. Are you going to Lady Severn's tonight to dinner?"

"Of course I am, and so are you. You know the famous prima donna, Mademoiselle Laurentia is staying at the Castle, and we shall hear her sing."

"Who is she? Another of old Lady Severn's *protégées*, I suppose. All her swans turn out geese. I only hope this one will not be a worse failure than usual."

"You at least, Noël, ought to be interested in Mademoiselle Laurentia, for she comes from your part of the world—from the backwoods of Canada."

"Really?" he questioned, with some show of interest at last.

"Yes; and Elsie Severn began to tell me some romantic story about her which I can't remember, for, just as she was at the most exciting part, Jones came in and related the account of the arrears in the Mackays' rent, and that put all Elsie's story out of my head."

"Yes, my dear, you have a faculty of remembering all the disagreeable things and forgetting all the pleasant ones. This adds much to your worth as a charming companion. I, who am honored with so much of your society, fully appreciate this quality."

Fortunately Lady Margaret did not hear this tender speech, for she was again deep in the recalcitrant Jones' accounts.

Let us glance for a moment at Noël McAllister, and see how years and prosperity have agreed with him. Lazily smoking in a comfortable arm-chair, this man is very different from the tall and slender youth we saw last on the pier at Rimouski.

He certainly had improved in appearance, and was a tall, fine-looking man of about five-and-thirty. He wore a light-colored tweed shooting suit, which contrasted well with his dark hair and bronzed complexion. A remarkably handsome man was The McAllister of Dunmorton, but to a close observer there was something lacking in his face—the old weakness about the mouth and chin, which time, instead of eradicating, had only served to develop. The hard school of adversity would have been a wholesome experience for Noël McAllister.

His life was not a busy one by any means: in fact, he spent most of his time in hunting or shooting, taking little interest in his tenants. After much persuasion from Lady Margaret, he had been induced to run for the county, and was returned unopposed, owing to the energetic canvassing of his wife, and the fact that most of the electors were his own tenants.

Poor Lady Margaret! she, indeed, had her trials. A woman of unbounded energy and ambition, she wished above all things that her husband should make his mark in the world. Vain hope!—a silent member in the House of Commons he was, and a silent member he would remain.

When he first arrived from Canada, ten years ago, his cousin anticipated great things from him. She saw his strong points as well as his weaknesses, and, being by some years his senior, hoped to mould him to her will. Alas! it was like beating against a stone wall—a wall of indifference and apathy.

McAllister had got his estate and the large revenue it yielded, and that was all he wanted. Lady Margaret was an appendage, and a very tiresome one into the bargain. She could not touch his sympathies, for whatever heart he ever had was far across the sea, where the cold green waters of the great St. Lawrence beat in unceasing murmur against the rocky beach at Father Point.

McAllister heard occasionally from his mother, whom he had often begged to come over to Scotland to share his prosperity, but the old lady always refused, saying that she was too old to venture so far from home.

He had written several times to M. Bois-le-Duc, but never had received any answer or news of the curé until a year ago, when a friar from Quebec had come to Scotland on a visit, and had brought a letter of introduction from the curé of Father Point to McAllister. The letter consisted only of a few short lines. Noël had often questioned his mother about Marie Gourdon, but on this subject the old lady was silent,—it is so easy to leave questions unanswered in letters.

"Margaret," Noël called out suddenly, rousing himself from his meditations, "I am going out now, and I shall not be back till five o'clock. I am going to ride up the Glen."

"Very well, but remember to be back in time to dress for dinner. Last time we were invited to the Severn's you were half an hour late, and Lady Severn has not forgiven you yet."

"Oh! all right. I shall be strictly on time this evening, and trust to make my peace with the old lady. Au revoir."

CHAPTER IX.

"Alas! our memories may retrace
Each circumstance of time and place;
Season and scene come back again,
And outward things unchanged remain:
The rest we cannot reinstate;
Ourselves we cannot re-create,
Nor get our souls to the same key
Of the remember'd harmony."

Longfellow.

The dinner party at Mount Severn this evening was an un-doubted success, as were most of Lady Severn's entertainments, for she possessed to a great degree that invaluable gift of a hostess—the art of allowing people to entertain themselves. And, added to the charm of her manner, and her undoubted tact in bringing the right people together, Lady Severn had all the accessories to make a dinner party go off well. The large dining-room was a long, low, octagonal apartment, with a small conservatory opening out at the lower end. There were numerous small alcoves in the wall, and in the recesses of each of these were huge pots of maidenhair fern.

All along the oak-panelled walls at short intervals were placed old-fashioned brass sconces with candles in them, which shed a clear though subdued light on the dinner table and the faces of the guests, and brought into prominence the bright hues of the ladies' gowns and the sparkling crystal and silver on the dinner table.

At the head of the table sat Lord Severn, a hale, hearty old gentleman of seventy. He was devoted to fox-hunting, and always ready to get up at five o'clock in the morning when a good run was in prospect. His wife sat opposite him. She was a beautiful old lady, her face clear-cut as a cameo. Her features were regular, and her bright black eyes flashed under her high intellectual forehead with a brilliancy a girl of sixteen might have envied. Her hair was snowy white, and rolled back *à la pompadour*.

Tonight she was dressed in a gown of heliotrope satin, trimmed with white point lace, and here and there in her hair and gown she wore pins made of the Severn diamonds. Round her neck glistened a magnificent necklace of these gems, which were of world-wide fame, having been given to Lord Severn by an Indian rajah as a recompense for saving him from drowning.

Lady Severn had been talking about her celebrated guest, who was not at dinner this evening.

"I am sorry you have not met Mademoiselle Laurentia; unfortunately she has been suffering for the last two days with a very severe nervous headache, and tonight did not feel inclined to come to dinner. However, I hope later on she will be better, and able to sing for you. Before dinner she went out into the garden, thinking the cool air would do her head good."

"Yes, I am very anxious to meet her," replied Lady Margaret, "and Noël is, for him, quite excited about her, coming as she does from Canada."

"Yes, she comes from Canada, and she has quite a romantic history. Perhaps she will tell you about that herself some day. She has only been with us a week, but already we are very fond of her, she is such a winning little creature, and her French Canadian songs are charming."

"Oh! Noël will be delighted," said Lady Margaret; "he waxes enthusiastic on the subject of French Canadian boat-songs. Do you think Mademoiselle Laurentia would spend a week with us at the Glen?"

"No, I'm afraid not; she is engaged to sing at Her Majesty's next week, and goes from here to London. You may have better luck in the autumn, though, when her London engagement is over."

"I'm sorry she can't come now, for we should have been delighted to have her at the Glen."

"Elsie dear," said Lady Severn to her daughter, a tall, fair girl of nineteen, who was endeavoring to amuse The McAllister, a difficult task—"Elsie dear, what part of Canada does Mademoiselle Laurentia come from?"

"Oh! somewhere on the banks of the St. Lawrence—some unpronounceable name."

"Delightfully vague," said Noël McAllister. "The ideas you English people have about our country are refreshing. One young lady, whom I supposed to have been fairly well educated, asked me, in the most matter-of-fact tone, whether we went down the rapids in toboggans. I can assure you it required a strong effort of will on my part to refrain from laughing outright."

"What did you tell her?" inquired Elsie.

"Oh! I said if she had ever seen either a rapid or a toboggan; she would hardly think of associating the two."

"Some day I wish you and Lady Margaret would make an excursion to Canada, and take me with you. It would be so exciting——"

"Come, Elsie," interrupted her mother, "come, we must go. Mademoiselle Laurentia will be lonely."

The ladies rose to go, Elsie saying in an undertone to The McAllister:

"Now, don't spend an hour over those stupid politics. I want you to hear mademoiselle sing."

"Politics!" he replied, with a disdainful shrug of his shoulders. "I take no interest whatever in them. Do not fear, Miss Elsie."

"I should like to know what you do take an interest in," remarked the young lady mischievously, as she hurried out of the room.

On entering the drawing-room they failed to find Mademoiselle Laurentia, so Lady Severn proposed that they should go into the garden.

"Elsie, run up to my room and fetch some shawls; the evening is quite chilly."

It was a lovely night in the end of April; the moon was full, and glimmering with sheeny whiteness over the distant hills. The garden at Mount Severn was an old-fashioned one, laid out in the early Elizabethan style in stately terraces and winding paths.

On each terrace were planted beds of luxuriant scarlet geraniums and early spring flowers. Every once in a while one came across a huge copper beech, and gloomy close-clipped hedges of yew divided the garden proper from the adjacent park.

Somewhere in the distance could be heard the trickling of a tiny rivulet, which supplied the fountain in the middle of the garden. There were many roughly-hewn, picturesque-looking rustic chairs scattered about, and near one of these Lady Margaret paused.

"May we sit here?" she said, turning to her hostess. "I really think this is the most delightful garden I ever saw in my life. They talk about Devonshire; I never saw anything half so lovely there."

"Yes, certainly it is pretty," assented its proprietress. "But where is Mademoiselle Laurentia?"

"In her favorite nook beside the old copper beech. See, you can catch a glimpse of her if you look round that tree."

Yes, there was Mademoiselle Laurentia, and a very insignificant little person she appeared at first sight. Her hands were clasped, and she was apparently deep in thought. She was clad in a gown of some soft shimmery white material, which fell in graceful folds about her, and in the clear beams of the moon looked like a robe of woven silver. Round her throat was a row of pearls, and in her dark brown hair were two or three diamond pins.

As Elsie Severn returned and came towards her, she lifted her head, and her face could be distinctly seen. A very sweet face it was, too, albeit not that of a woman in the first freshness of her youth.

The eyes were dark and bright, the forehead broad and low, with lines of strong determination marked on it. The mouth, that most characteristic feature, was somewhat large and expressive. But the successful prima donna's face wore a not altogether happy expression, though when she spoke the sad look went out of it; only when in repose it was always there.

"Well, Mademoiselle Laurentia, how is your head now? Better, I hope?"

"Yes, dear, the pain is quite gone now. And how did your dinner-party go off?"

"Oh! very well. I sat next The McAllister, and he was a little more lively than usual. He is most anxious to meet you. You know he comes from Canada."

"Yes, I know," said Mademoiselle Laurentia abruptly.

"Did you ever meet him there?" went on Elsie.

"I used to know a family called McAllister a long time ago, when I was quite young."

"Indeed? But, mademoiselle, don't talk as if you were a hundred. I'm sure you don't look much older than I."

"In years, perhaps, I am not so very much older; but in thought, Elsie, a century."

"Poor Mademoiselle Laurentia, your life has been a hard one, in spite of all its success. I don't want to intrude, but I often think you must have had some great sorrow. Have you?"

"Yes, my dear, I have. I cannot talk of it tonight, though. No, no, not tonight at any rate."

Elsie rather wondered why she laid such particular stress on the present time, but did not like to pursue the subject.

"Elsie, would you like me to sing for you now?" asked Mademoiselle Laurentia suddenly. "This garden is an inspiration."

"Yes, I should, above all things, if you feel well enough."

"Then what shall it be? Choose."

"Oh! if you please, Gounod's Slumber-song. This is just the time and place for it."

Accordingly, with only the rippling of the fountain as an accompaniment, the sweet clear notes rose, and the highly-trained voice of the prima donna performed the difficult runs and trills of this most beautiful of slumber-songs with that precision and delicacy attained by years of practice and hard training.

The song came to an end, and for a few moments no one spoke, till at length Elsie Severn, drawing a deep sigh of relief, said in her impulsive way:

"Why, Mademoiselle Laurentia, I have never heard you sing like that before. I thought I had heard you at your best in London, but I never *felt* your singing so much as tonight."

"I am glad you were pleased, my dear. Would you like another?"

"Yes, above all things. Just wait a moment though; I want to speak to mamma."

Elsie crossed over to where Lady Severn sat, and whispered to her saying:

"If the gentlemen come out while mademoiselle is singing, don't let any of them come over to us. She can't bear a crowd round her, and I don't want her to be disturbed."

"Very well, child; it shall be as you wish. I hope, though, you did not ask mademoiselle to sing; you must not do that."

"No, no, indeed I did not, mamma. She offered to sing for me."

A curious friendship had sprung up last winter in London between Elsie Severn and the famous prima donna. They had met one afternoon at a reception, and been mutually pleased with each other. There was something about the frank outspoken manner of the young girl which appealed to Mademoiselle Laurentia, wearied as she was with the conventional adulation, in reality amounting to so little, of the world in which she moved.

"Now, mademoiselle," said Elsie, "I am ready. It is so good of you to sing for me."

"My child, you know I love to give you pleasure," she replied, stroking the girl's fair hair caressingly. "Listen! I will sing for you a song I have not sung for years—ah! so many, many years."

She began softly, slowly, a Canadian boat-song, heard often on the raftsman's barge or habitant's canoe, on the Ottawa or great St. Lawrence—a national song, with its quaint monotonous melody and simple pathetic words.

And the voice which rendered so effectively the technical difficulties of Wagner and Gounod sang this simple air with a pathos and feeling all its own:

> *"A la claire fontaine*
> *M'en allant promener,*
> *J'ai trouvé l'eau si belle*
> *Que je me suis baigné.*
> *Il y a longtemps que je t'aime*
> *Jamais je ne t'oublierai.*
> *Il y a longtemps que je t'aime*
> *Jamais je ne t'oublierai."*

"Why, McAllister, whatever is the matter with you? Have you seen a ghost? You are as white as a sheet. Are you ill?"

"No, no, I'm not ill. Do be quiet, Jack. What a row you're making! I do feel a little seedy; it's these horrid cigars of yours."

"Nonsense!" retorted Jack Severn. "You couldn't get better ones; it isn't that. I believe you've seen the ghost of old Lady Severn, my great-grandmother, walking with her head in her hands. This is the time of year she always turns up. It must be the spring house-cleaning that disturbs her rest. *Did* you see her? I've sat up night after night to try and catch sight of the old lady, and I've always missed her. Where was she? Tell me quickly. I'll run after her."

"I didn't see your great-grandmother or anybody else, so do stop chattering, Jack, and for goodness' sake let me hear that song," said McAllister irritably.

"Well, well," muttered Jack Severn to himself, "I never saw The McAllister in such a temper before. As a rule, he is too lazy to be angry at anything, I really think he must be ill."

Mademoiselle Laurentia finished singing. The McAllister's thoughts by this time were far away on the pebbly beach at Father Point, where the tide was coming in rippling over the stones, and his memory had gone back to an evening ten years ago. He was again standing beside a huge boulder, on which sat a girl in a pink cotton frock. She was singing in a sweet low voice:

> *"Il y a longtemps que je t'aime,*
> *Jamais je ne t'oublierai."*

And he was saying to her:
"Marie, you know, my dear one—

> *'Il y a longtemps que je t'aime.'*

Yes, for years. My love for you is deep as that great river, and stronger, mightier." And the girl had answered, looking at him with her great brown eyes full of unutterable tenderness and faith:

"Yes, Noël, I believe you will never change;" and their voices joined in the refrain of that old boat-song, awaking the echoes:

"Il y a longtemps que je t'aime,
Jamais je ne t'oublierai."

"Mr. McAllister, how ill you look," said Elsie Severn, coming towards him, and noticing his weary, abstracted expression.

"Yes, that's just what I was saying," put in the irrepressible Jack. "I think he'd better go home."

"How rude you are!" said his sister. "Come, Mr. McAllister, come into the house, and I will give you a cup of tea. That will do you good, and then I will introduce you to Mademoiselle Laurentia."

"Oh! Miss Elsie, there's nothing the matter with me. I should like to be introduced to Mademoiselle Laurentia now."

"Very well. See, she is coming this way," said Elsie. "Is she not pretty? Have you ever seen her before?"

"Seen her before? How could I have seen her before?"

He told the untruth unblushingly; it was by no means his first.

Mademoiselle Laurentia was close to them now, and Elsie

said, in her clear, distinct tones:

"Let me introduce Mr. McAllister to you, mademoiselle. You are compatriots."

Just then Lady Severn called Elsie, and Marie Gourdon and Noël McAllister were left alone for a moment. She was the first to break the awkward silence, as she said in her quiet voice, without the faintest shade of embarrassment in it:

"How do you like this country, Mr. McAllister?"

"How do I like this country? Is that all you have to say to me after these years?"

"What else can I have to say to you? Is not this a fine old garden? How brightly the moon shines!"

"Marie Gourdon, do not speak to me in that calm, aggravating way. Reproach me! Anything but this. I cannot bear your indifference."

"Reproach you? For what? Do you mean for leaving me? If so, that is an old story, told long, long ago. I am thankful now you did leave me. And, Mr. McAllister, I must remind you that only to my most intimate friends am I known as Marie Gourdon. I must beg you to excuse me now; Lady Severn is calling me."

CHAPTER X.

"O! primavera gioventù dell' anno!
O! gioventù primavera della vitæ!!!"

It was a beautiful afternoon in the middle of June, and the London season was at its height. Everyone who was anybody of importance was now in town. Sweet, fresh-looking girls, in the full enjoyment of their first season, were cantering by, gaily chattering in the Row, their faces glowing with excitement and pleasure as they caught sight of some pedestrian acquaintances and nodded their greetings. Stately old dowagers were enjoying to the full the bright sunshine, as they lay comfortably back in their well-padded broughams. Here were brilliantly apparelled men and women, the very butterflies of London society, talking of the events of yesterday, and speculating on the evening's entertainment, as they walked leisurely up and down the broad promenade of the Park. But near, and almost touching the skirts of these favored ones, ran an undercurrent of poverty, distress and misery. So close allied were the two streams of human life, that scarce an arm's length divided them.

Here and there, just outside the Park gates, were pale, emaciated women and young girls, in whom was left no youth, for in truth their hard lives had served to age them before their time. With thin, white hands they stretched out their offerings of flowers to sell the passer-by—bright spring flowers—crocuses, daffodils and violets, whose freshness and purity served only to enhance the miserable aspect of their vendors. In verity it was a scene of velvet and rags, satin and sackcloth, riches and poverty: Lazarus looking longingly at Dives, and Dives going on his way unheeding.

At the marble arch entrance to the Park there stood this afternoon a tall, rather melancholy looking man, dressed in deep mourning. He was watching, with apparently little interest, the busy throng about them. From time to time he lifted his hat in a mechanical manner as he recognized some acquaintance, but there was nothing enthusiastic in his greetings. He had been standing at the entrance for about half-an-hour, when he was roused from his state of abstraction by a tremendous slap on the back, and a sturdy voice, which said:

"Hello! McAllister, old boy, how are you? Why are you star-gazing here? Wake up, old boy, wake up!"

"Oh! Jack, how are you?" said McAllister, for he it was, turning round sharply. "I'm glad to see you. I thought you were in France."

"Well, so I was, but the fellow I went with couldn't speak a word of French, and you know I can't. We started on this walking tour through the Pyrenees, where no English is spoken. The consequence was that we were nearly starved—couldn't make the people understand. I got tired of making signs, as if I were a deaf mute, so I just turned back and came home, and here I am."

"How are Lady Severn and Miss Elsie?"

"Both very well, thank you. Elsie is enjoying her season thoroughly. I never saw such a girl before in my life. She is out morning, noon and night. I declare she tires me out, and I can't begin to keep pace with her. One ball at nine, another at ten; rush, rush, all the time, it is terrible. She has the constitution of a horse, I believe."

"Not very complimentary to Miss Elsie," said Noël laughing.

"True, nevertheless. I say, McAllister, you look very glum. What is the matter with you? Oh! ah! I beg your pardon, I—I— What an ass I am, always putting my foot into it. Pray forgive me."

"Yes," said Noël, "it was very sad. You know, Lady Margaret always would drive those ponies; we could not prevent her. She was determined to break them in, and, when she decided on a thing, she always carried her point. That morning, she drove to the Glen; the precipice there is very steep, and something frightened the ponies, and—and you know the rest."

"Yes, yes," said Jack shuddering, "I heard it all. I am very sorry for you, old boy. Lady Margaret was very kind to me. She used to scold me occasionally, but I expect I deserved it. No, no, don't talk about it any more. You must cheer up, old boy. Come with me to the opera tonight. Mademoiselle Laurentia is going to sing in 'Aida.'"

"Mademoiselle Laurentia?"

"Yes, don't you remember her? She was up at Mount Severn last autumn."

"Oh, yes! I remember her well enough; but, Jack, I can't go to the opera, much as I should like it. You see it would not look well," touching the crape band on his hat.

"No, no, of course not," said Jack hurriedly; "pray pardon me, how stupid I am; but I know what we can do. I have tickets for a conversazione at the Academy tomorrow—there can be no harm in your going to that. I hear there are some very good things at the Academy this year."

"Yes, so I heard, I have not been there yet."

"Every one is in ecstasies over a painting by a man called Lacroix; they say it's the best thing that has been on view for a long time."

"What! painted by a man called Eugène Lacroix? Does he come from Father Point?"

"Yes. My dear McAllister, you Canadians are having it all your own way in London this year. Whether it is this Colonial Exhibition, or whether you are all extremely gifted people, I don't know."

"What is Eugène Lacroix like?" asked The McAllister. "I used to know him a long time ago. He was a quiet sort of man then."

"He is quiet yet. He won't go out anywhere, but works, works all the time. Sometimes he comes to tea at my mother's on Sunday afternoon, but that is the only time we see anything of him. Mademoiselle Laurentia introduced him to us. All the Academy people speak well of him, strange to say, for he is a foreigner, and they are prejudiced against outsiders, as a rule. He has had several things hung at the *Salon* in Paris, and a head he painted of Mademoiselle Laurentia made a great hit last spring. But, old boy, I must be going now, I've got to take Elsie to a dinner party tonight. Fearful bore, but when duty calls me, I always obey. You'll come with me tomorrow, eh? Then just drive round to the house at two o'clock sharp. Au revoir."

"Stop a moment, Jack. Can you give me Mademoiselle Laurentia's address?"

"Yes, certainly, Number 17, The Grove Highgate. Are you going to see her? It always struck me that you and she didn't get on very well last autumn at Mount Severn."

"Did it strike you in that way?"

"Yes, it did, and I couldn't help noticing that whenever you came in one door she seemed to go out of the other; in fact, old boy, I'm sure she didn't like you much."

"Are you?"

"Yes, and Elsie thought just as I do."

"Indeed, you are wonderfully observant, Jack. I did not credit you with such powers of perspicacity."

"I don't know what you mean by that, but I can see through a stone wall as well as any one else, though I was always very stupid at school."

"Well, perhaps what you say may be true, Jack, but I'm going to call on Mademoiselle Laurentia. You know we Canadians are very patriotic."

"I admire you for your forgiving disposition. If you really want to see Mademoiselle Laurentia, the only time to catch her in is between five and six. Good-bye, old fellow, I must be off. Don't forget tomorrow at two o'clock sharp."

After Jack went, McAllister hesitated for a moment, then glanced at his watch, hailed a passing hansom, jumped in, and called out to the driver, "Go to 17, The Grove, Highgate. A sovereign if you get there before six o'clock."

The cabman shook his head doubtfully and said, "I'll try my best, sir, but I'm afraid I can't do it. It's a long way off, you know."

He did try his best at any rate, and off they went at break-neck speed, on! on! on! past rows and rows of houses, past wildernesses of brick and mortar. Far behind them they left churches, hospitals, buildings innumerable, the mansions of the rich and the wretched dwellings of the poor, the squalid habitations of outcast London, on! on! on! Up the great hill of Highgate, where the tender green foliage of early summer and of the great oak trees bordered the roadside, and where the almond blossoms perfumed all the heated air with a subtle delicate fragrance, on! on! on!

Quickly they dashed past many an historic spot, past the house where Coleridge lived, past the walls of the great cemetery, which contains the ashes of hundreds of illustrious dead, past the little church, perched on the summit of the hill, from whose belfry could be heard the chimes for evensong, coming faintly on the still air; on! on! on!

But it is a long lane that has no turning, and at length the hansom drew up before a little cottage far back from the road. A long porch of lattice-work led up to the front door, and tall elm trees shaded the little garden. It was a pleasant enough little abode on the outside at any rate, sheltered from the noise and bustle of the great city.

"No. 17, The Grove, sir," called out the cabman, breathless, but triumphant, "and it's only five minutes to six."

"Well done," said McAllister, "here's your well-earned sovereign. Now take your horse to the stables over there and wait for me."

The cabman departed radiant, wondering over such unwonted generosity, and musing as to the rank and wealth of his fare.

McAllister knocked at the door of the cottage, and presently it was opened by a neat maid-servant, who, in answer to his inquiry, said:

"I am afraid, sir, Mademoiselle Laurentia will not be able to see you. What name shall I say, please, sir?"

"Oh, say I'm a Canadian. I have no cards with me; but I have come on a matter of the utmost importance, and I must see your mistress."

"Very well, sir; please walk up this way," and the maid led the way to Mademoiselle Laurentia's boudoir.

It was a dainty little room furnished in blue and silver. On the walls hung numerous water-colors and engravings, showing that the prima donna had an artistic eye.

McAllister had not long to wait before the mistress of the house came in. She was dressed for her part in "Aida," and wore an Egyptian robe of soft white cashmere, embroidered in dull gold silk with a quaint conventional pattern. Her gown was slightly open at the throat, round which was a necklace of dull gold beads. Heavy bracelets of the same material encircled her arms, and a row of them held back her dark brown hair, which fell in heavy masses far below her knees.

She came into the room with her hands stretched out in welcome, but at the sight of McAllister drew back looking surprised.

"How do you do, Mr. McAllister," she said, in a formal tone. "This is indeed an unexpected pleasure. Pray pardon my theatrical dress, but I have such a long drive into town that I am obliged to dress early."

"Certainly, Marie; your dress is very becoming; in fact, you look altogether charming."

"Mr. McAllister, before you speak again, I think I may tell you that once before I have had to remind you that only to my most intimate friends am I known as Marie Gourdon."

"Am I not your friend? I have known you all your life."

"I do not wish to continue that subject; and pardon me, Mr. McAllister, if I seem rude, but it is now past six o'clock, and I must leave here in twenty minutes. It is a long drive into town, and I must be at the opera on time."

"I have something very important to say to you. My wife is dead."

"What! Lady Margaret dead? I am really very sorry to hear that. She was always very kind to me. Poor Lady Margaret."

"And do you know, Marie, what her death means to me?"

"No, I don't quite follow you, Mr. McAllister. You say your wife is dead, I suppose you *mean* she is dead."

"Yes, yes, of course," replied Noël irritably, "but it means more. It means that I am free."

"Free! What do you mean?"

"Marie, can you ask me that? Can you pretend not to understand? For the last ten years my life has been a burden to me. The thought of you has ever been with me. The memories of Father Point, of the happy days spent there, haunt me always. And now, Marie, I have come to tell you that Dunmorton is yours, the Glen is yours, all that I have is yours, and Marie *I* am yours."

During this outburst Marie Gourdon's face grew at first crimson, then very white, and for a moment she did not answer; then she rose from her chair, and, looking straight at The McAllister, said in a very quiet tone, without the faintest touch of anger in it:

"Noël McAllister, you are strangely mistaken in me. Do you think I am exactly the same person I was ten years ago? Do you think I am the same little country girl whose heart you won so easily and threw aside when better prospects offered?"

"Marie, it was you who bade me go."

"Yes, I bade you go. What else could I do? I saw you wished to be free. I saw that my feelings, yes—if you will have the truth—my love for you weighed as nothing in the scale against your newly-found fortune. I saw you waver, hesitate. *I* did not hesitate. And now I am rich, I am famous, you come to me. You offer me that worthless thing,—your love. When I was poor, struggling alone, friendless, did you even write to me? Did you by word or look recognize me? No! The farce is played out. I wonder at your coming to see me after all."

"Marie, listen; a word——"

"No, not one word, Noël McAllister. I have said all I shall ever say to you. Dunmorton, the Glen, all your possessions are very fine things, but there are others I value infinitely more. Dear me! is that half-past six striking? I believe I hear the carriage at the door. I must beg of you to excuse me. You know my duties are pressing, and managers wait for no one. Good-evening, Mr. McAllister."

CHAPTER XI.

"Because thou hast believed the wheels of life
Stand never idle, but go always round;
Hast labored, but with purpose; hast become
Laborious, persevering, serious, firm—
For this thy track across the fretful foam
Of vehement actions without scope or term,
Call'd history, keeps a splendor, due to wit,
Which saw one clue to life and followed it."

Matthew Arnold.

The day so long anxiously looked for of the great reception at the Royal Academy came at last. Fortunately the weather was beautiful, and the sun shone on the London streets with an unusual brightness even for that time of year.

Long rows of carriages lined the streets approaching the entrance to the Academy. The great staircase leading into the main hall was carpeted with crimson baize, for Royal visitors were expected, and on each stair were placed luxuriant pots of hothouse plants which perfumed the heated air with an almost overpowering fragrance.

As the lucky possessors of invitation cards passed in, a footman resplendent in crimson and gold livery handed each a catalogue of the pictures.

What a motley throng it was! Bohemia rubbing shoulders with orthodox conventionality. Duchesses, actors, artists, bishops, newspaper men out at elbows, deans, girl art students, spruce looking Eton boys in tall hats and short jackets, all eagerly pushing their way to the envied goal. A frantic endeavor it was, too. To tell the truth, few of the throng came to see the pictures; most of them, firmly believing that "the proper study of mankind is man," assembled to view each other. Of course there were some conscientious art critics, but these were few and far between.

The Gallery rapidly filled, and the guests by degrees formed themselves into little groups.

Four or five men of the most Bohemian type were gathered in front of a large canvas hung on the line, an enviable position. They were all foreigners, and were attracting much attention by their shrill voices and gesticulations. "Yes," said one, a little Frenchman, "I know he's not an Englishman, no Englishman ever painted like that. No, I should think not. The tone, the purity, the—the——"

"No, he's not an Englishman," said a representative of the British nation passing just then, and pausing to take up the cudgels for his country. "He's not an Englishman, but I don't like your prejudice; he's not a Frenchman either, for that matter, so you can't claim him."

"What is he, then?" demanded the little Frenchman.

"He's a Canadian."

"Canadian, ah! What's his name?"

"Lacroix."

"Oh! he's half French at any rate," said the little artist triumphantly, "and I know he studied in Paris. Well, this is a masterpiece I know, no matter who painted it."

The picture which had caused so much discussion was a very large one, covering some five feet of canvas. In the foreground was a long sandy road, on which was a procession of all manner of vehicles of different kinds. Hay-carts, calashes, buck-boards, and rude specimens of cabs were being driven by French-Canadian habitants along the road. In the middle distance was a churchyard crowded with people, most of them looking very ill, and many of them leaning on crutches. The invalids seemed to be attended by their relatives or friends, whose strongly-knit frames and sunburned faces contrasted vividly with those of the pilgrims.

The wonderful thing about this picture was the distinct manner with which each of the many faces was brought out on the canvas. In a marvellous way, too, the interior of the church just beyond the graveyard was portrayed. Through the door, flung widely open, and crowded with an eager multitude, could be seen the High Altar, the candles brightly burning in honor of the Holy Sacrament, and at the rail were lines of pilgrims awaiting the approach of the officiating priest.

The priest, an imposing figure clad in the gorgeous vestments of the Roman Catholic church, was bending down and allowing the worshippers to touch a relic of the Good St. Anne, in whose miraculous power of healing they so firmly trusted.

A well-put together picture, the critics said, and a new scene which in these days is much to be desired. The manner in which Lacroix had arranged to show both the exterior and interior of the church was a clever hit, every one agreed. Outside, with the clear blue sky for background, the spire of the church was clearly defined, and on a niche just above the main doorway stood an exquisitely carved statue of the patron St. Anne, holding by the hand her little daughter, the Blessed Virgin. And beyond the church and the mass of sorrowing, suffering human life at its doors was the great River St. Lawrence, a molten silver stream glimmering with a million iridescent lights, flowing swiftly, silently on.

Far across its broad expanse, in the dim distance, like huge clouds, were the misty blue Laurentian hills, grand, eternal, steadfast, an emblem of Omnipotence itself.

"Where is the painter of this masterpiece?" asked one; and a friend of his, a Royal Academician of some standing, replied:

"Oh! Lacroix has just come in. The prince admired 'The Pilgrimage' and inquired for the artist, so the president sent for him. The prince was most affable to him, and, it is said, has bought the picture. Ah! there is Lacroix now. Wait a moment and I will bring him over here."

Presently he returned with Lacroix, who was enthusiastically received by his fellow artists, and congratulated heartily on his success. Lacroix was a tall, rather uncouth-looking man of between thirty-five and forty, and his face wore a stern, care-worn expression. But, to an observer who cared to study his countenance, over the stern gravity of the artist's face there was often a gleam of pleasing expression, more particularly when lighted up by one of his rare smiles. Today he did not seem very much elated by his success; rather the contrary. Success had come to Lacroix too late in life for him to have any very jubilant feeling about it. It seemed that he had long out-lived his youth, its hopes and ambitions. Work was what he lived for now, work and his art; if success followed, well and good; if not, he did not much care.

"Yes," he said, in a voice with a slight French accent, in reply to some question they had asked him, "I studied in Paris, then I came to London last year, and have been here ever since; but, I may say, I received all my training in France."

"Ah! I thought so," said the little French artist. "Your style is too good for the English school. You are a Canadian, I hear. We have a good many Canadians in London this year. I went to hear one sing last night at Her Majesty's, Mademoiselle Laurentia. Do you know her? I can assure you she is superb. She is a Canadian, too."

"I did know her many, years ago," said Lacroix; "but I have seldom seen her of late; in fact, I don't think she would remember me now."

"She is here today, I am told," said the little Frenchman, looking round the gallery. "Ah! there she is talking to Lady D——. See, there, that little lady in grey!"

Lacroix glanced in the direction indicated. Was that fashionable little lady conversing completely at her ease with one of the highest in the land indeed Marie Gourdon, the daughter of the fisherman at Father Point? Yes; there was no mistaking her, and he wondered a little whether Marie had changed mentally as much as her outward circumstances had altered.

"So, you did know the prima donna before?" went on the little French artist.

"Oh! yes; we are both natives of Father Point, on the Lower St. Lawrence."

"Indeed, how interesting. Remain here a moment, and I shall ask Mademoiselle Laurentia to come over and look at your picture;" and the little man dashed off impulsively, and, detaching the prima donna from Lady D——, brought her over to the spot where Eugène was standing.

No; she had not forgotten him, for she held out her hand and shook his warmly, saying, in the frank, sympathetic voice he remembered so well:

"I am very glad, indeed, to see you, M. Lacroix. Let me add my congratulations to the many you have already received. Your picture is indeed a masterpiece."

"Thank you. You are, I suppose, the only one here today who can say whether my picture is true to nature."

"Yes, indeed, I can; it takes me back to the old days at Father Point, and how real it all is! There is M. Bois-le-Duc, dear M. Bois-le-Duc. I can almost fancy I am standing on the road watching the pilgrims go into the church."

"I am glad you like it. By the way, I heard from M. Bois-le-Duc by yesterday's mail. He wrote me a long letter this time. Would you like to read it?"

"Yes, very much," said the prima donna, eagerly; "very much, indeed."

"I think I have it here," searching hurriedly through his numerous pockets. "Ah! no; but I shall send it to you."

"Why not bring it, M. Lacroix?"

"May I?"

"Yes. I shall be very pleased to see you as well as the letter," said mademoiselle, smiling graciously. "I am always at home at five o'clock. You know my address, number 17, The Grove, Highgate."

"Thanks, I will come tomorrow, with your permission. My time in London, you know, is very short, for I sail for Canada the first week of next month."

"Indeed, so soon? How I envy you. I am sorry you are going, though. Good-bye for the present, I must go back to Lady D——. Remember, five o'clock tomorrow."

"Au revoir, mademoiselle. I shall see you tomorrow."

Mademoiselle Laurentia had not left him many moments before the president crossed the room to where he was standing, and said in a cordial tone:

"My dear Lacroix, I am happy to tell you that the prince has bought your picture."

"'The Pilgrimage,' do you mean?"

"Yes, yes; you don't seem very delighted about it."

"Well," said Lacroix, "the fact is that I shall miss it. It has been part of my life for the last four years. Oh! yes, I shall miss it."

"But, my dear Lacroix, do be practical. Just think of the price you will get. Think, too, of the *éclat*. What a queer unworldly sort of creature you are. Any other man would be fairly beside himself with joy at such success as yours."

"Yes," replied Lacroix, wearily; "of course I know it is a great thing for me. I appreciate it, indeed I do."

"You do not show your appreciation very enthusiastically," said the president, as he moved off to speak to some other guests who were just coming into the gallery.

Next day, early in the afternoon, Lacroix started for his long walk up Highgate Hill, with M. Bois-le-Duc's letter safely in his pocket this time. He was a good walker and used to outdoor exercise, and enjoyed the prospect of the long tramp this bright summer day.

He did not hurry himself, for there was plenty of time before five o'clock, and he stopped every few moments to examine some wayside plant, and to listen with the ardor of a true lover of nature to the merry voices of the thrush and blackbird singing a gladsome carol.

And he was often tempted by the fascinating beauty of the quiet landscape, as he left the grimy smoke of London far behind him and ascended into the pure fresh country, to take out his sketch-book and dot down dainty little glimpses, thus laying up a store for future work.

But at length he reached number 17, The Grove, and the door was opened by the trim little maid-servant, who replied, in answer to his inquiry—

"Yes, sir, Mademoiselle Laurentia is at home. Please walk up this way."

CHAPTER XII.

"I know, dear heart! that in our lot
May mingle tears and sorrow;
But love's rich rainbow's built from tears
Today, with smiles tomorrow.
The sunshine from our sky may die,
The greenness from life's tree,
But ever 'mid the warring storm
Thy nest shall shelter'd be.
The world may never know, dear heart!
What I have found in thee;
But, though naught to the world, dear heart!
Thou'rt all the world to me."

Gerald Massey.

Mademoiselle Laurentia was sitting at her five o'clock tea-table, a dainty little wicker-work affair, covered with delicate china of palest pink, blue and green tints. The cups and saucers were clustered invitingly round a huge old-fashioned silver tea-pot, and, on the nob of the little fire-place a kettle was singing away merrily. A great rug of white bear-skin was stretched on the floor, and curled up comfortably in its warmest corner lay a large Persian cat, which, at the entrance of the visitor, merely turned languidly to see whether he had a dog, and then sank into sleep again.

A very homelike scene it was that Eugène Lacroix was ushered upon that summer afternoon, and the greeting of his hostess set him at once at his ease.

"How do you feel, Mr. Lacroix, today, after all your triumphs yesterday? You received quite an ovation at the reception."

"Oh, I feel very well, indeed, thank you; this fresh country air puts new life into one. You were wise, mademoiselle, to choose your home in such a spot."

"Yes, I think I did well, though the place has its drawbacks. It is a long way from London and the opera. Still, I could not bear to live quite in town; the air there stifles me. After the clear bracing air of Canada, I find London very oppressive. But, M. Lacroix, you must be tired after your long walk up the hill. Do take that comfortable arm-chair and let me give you a cup of tea."

"Yes, gladly; tea is one of my weaknesses. Oh! how I missed it in Paris. It is almost impossible to get a good cup of tea there."

"I always make mine myself, and have it regularly at five o'clock, and, even now, I still keep the fire lighted here, for the evenings are apt to be chilly, and I have to take care of my throat. That is *my* fortune, you know."

"Yes, it is indeed, mademoiselle. How strange that all three of the curé's pupils should have succeeded so well in life, and all so far from their own land."

"It is indeed strange. That thought has often occurred to me, too," said Marie, musingly.

"But," went on Lacroix, "though, of course, I like London and Paris and all this excitement for a time, I often pine for our fresh Canadian breezes, for the dash of the Gulf against the rocks at Father Point! City life is so trammelled, and I long for the unconventional home life from which I have been removed so long."

"Ah! I see you have *mal de pays*; you see I know the symptoms," said Marie, smiling.

"Yes, I suppose it must be that."

"But how delighted you must be at the success of your picture. I saw by this morning's paper that it was bought by the prince."

"Of course, I am glad of my success. True, it has come late in life; but still it *has* come. But I shall miss my picture very much."

"Naturally."

"However, I shall soon see the reality again. I am going home for a holiday next month."

"Indeed? How I envy you."

"Yes, I am really going, and I am counting the days until it is time to sail. But, mademoiselle, I am forgetting to show you M. Bois-le-Duc's letter. I have it with me; shall I leave it here?"

"No, M. Lacroix. I am very lazy this afternoon, and if you would read it to me while I just sit in this comfortable arm-chair and do nothing but listen, I should enjoy that above all things."

"Certainly, mademoiselle; nothing would please me better. I imagine your days of laziness, as you call it, are few and far between. Now, I will begin. The letter is dated Father Point, April 20th, 1887:—

"My Dear Eugène,

"I was very pleased to receive your last letter, and more than pleased to hear of your success; but the news that delighted me most of all was to hear that you were coming here this summer.

"What you tell me about my brother is very satisfactory; I knew he would be kind to you. I like to think of you as you describe yourself sitting in the great hall of the Hôtel Bois-le-Duc, in Paris, where I spent so many happy days. I knew you and the marquise would have many subjects in common, and, as you say, she is one of the ladies of the old school, now alas! past, yet she can sympathize with Bohemianism, provided that talent is allied with it. She is a woman good as she is charming, and highly cultivated. True, I have not seen my sister-in-law for years, but her letters to me are as clever and interesting as those of Madame de Stael, and I know from them how her mind, instead of being dimmed with advancing years, has developed with every day.

"Your description of the old garden, with its rippling fountains and quaint *parterres*, reminds me of the days of my youth, when my mother gave her receptions there. Yes, my dear pupil, the halls of that old house and the old-fashioned garden have been the scene of many gay gatherings in the olden time, when France had a true aristocracy. And not only stately dames and courtiers thronged to the Hôtel Bois-le-Duc, but the foremost minds of the day lent brilliancy to my mother's *salons*. Wits, authors, poets, artists, statesmen, whose words could change the fate of Europe, were proud to call the marquise friend. I am an old man now, and you must forgive an old man's prosiness; but a little sadness comes into my thoughts when I muse on the past. How many of those illustrious souls, then so full of life and power, remain? And I, long exiled from all I cherished, how have I progressed? No, no, Eugène; not even to you would I complain. What has a faithful follower of the Cross to do with the vanities of this world?

"It is one of my temptations, still, to think on what might have been had I not chosen the hard road, had I not renounced the gay world and its fascinations, for it had, and *has* fascinations yet for me. Eugène, my reward will be hereafter; but, as an old man, and one who has endeavored to do his duty for many years, I often wonder whether I mistook my vocation. But away with such doubts, they are a snare of the arch-enemy himself, a subtle snare.

"My dear pupil, hard as it was to let you go, I am glad you left me. I knew those years of labor *must* tell in the end. I knew so much zeal could not be thrown away.

"Of Marie Gourdon, all you tell me is most satisfactory. When first I sent her to fight her way in the world, I had fears. In her profession there are so many evil influences to contend with that, in spite of her undoubted talent, I hesitated before letting her go. But I need not have feared. Marie Gourdon has one of those pure white souls—"

"Perhaps I had better not go on?" said Eugène, smiling.

Marie nodded and murmured half to herself—"Dear M. Bois-le-Duc, I am glad to hear he thinks so well of me. Please continue."

"—one of those pure white souls that can pass through the fire of any temptation and come out purer, stronger, holier. She has doubly repaid me for any pains I took with her education. Long ago she insisted on returning the money spent on her training, and every year regularly, she sends me two hundred dollars to be spent on the poor suffering pilgrims, who come to the church at Father Point. Yes, I am justly proud of two of my pupils; the disappointment I suffer because of the conduct of the third only serves to heighten the contrast. I beg of you never to mention his name again to me. Never allude to Noël McAllister in your letters in the slightest way. The manner in which he treated—"

Here Lacroix hesitated, grew very red and lost his place.

Marie, observing his distress, remarked placidly: "Please go on, I do not mind; that is all a closed page in my history."

"The manner in which he treated," continued Lacroix, "that poor girl was unpardonable. At an age, too, when she should have been most carefully guarded, when her feelings were most sensitive, he, for all he knew to the contrary, broke her heart. And, under the cowardly pretense that it was she who bade him go, he left her to live, for aught he cared, a dreary, colorless existence at Father Point.

"Fortunately Marie was a girl of no ordinary stamp. She could rise above disappointments—remember, I do not say forget them; and she threw her whole energies into her art. I am a priest, and know human nature, its weakness and its strength—and human nature is the same all the world over—and I can honestly say that the daughter of the fisherman at Father Point is the noblest woman I have ever met.

"I can feel no interest in what you tell me of Noël McAllister. As I said before, I do not wish you to mention him. Madame McAllister died last week, very calmly and peacefully. We laid her in the churchyard beside her husband and his ancestors. She had been very frail of late years, but of course she was a great age, ninety-six.

"You will scarcely know Father Point when you return. An enterprising merchant from Montreal has built a large summer hotel on the Point, and hopes to attract crowds of visitors during the warm weather.

"Of course you have heard of the honor conferred on our Archbishop. I went up to Quebec to attend the ceremony when they gave him his Cardinal's hat, and he is soon to visit my humble parish, and I trust will approve of our progress, both in things spiritual and temporal.

"Hoping to see you soon, and with every good wish for your safe voyage,

"Believe me, as ever,

"Your very sincere friend,

"Réné Bois-le-Duc,

"Curé of Father Point, Province of Quebec, Canada."

"Dear M. Bois-le-Duc," repeated Marie, "I am glad he thinks so well of me. The approval of one true friend like that is worth more than all the applause I get night after night at the opera. He knows me for myself; they only recognize my art and the pleasure it affords them."

"Yes; you were always a first favorite with the curé," said Lacroix.

"How angry he is with Noël McAllister; needlessly so. *I* have forgiven him long ago."

"Have you, indeed? And have you heard about Lady Margaret?"

"Yes. Mr. McAllister did me the honor of calling on me the other day."

"Noël McAllister called on you, Marie?"

The old name slipped out accidentally, and, in his excitement, he did not notice the mistake.

"Yes."

"And he told you about Lady Margaret, about his wife being dead?"

"Yes."

"Was that all he told you?"

Marie looked rather surprised at being cross-questioned in this abrupt manner; but replied quietly:—

"No; it was not all. He told me much more."

"Yes! yes!" said Lacroix, with the persistency of a cross-examining lawyer, "And you Marie, what did you say?"

"If you really want to know exactly what I said, my words were to the effect that I had no time to reopen a closed chapter in my life, and that my carriage was at the door."

A strange expression, almost of relief, with surprise mingled, crossed the artist's grave face, and he did not speak for a moment. Then he said, slowly, in a tone of half-pitying contempt:

"Poor McAllister! What with you and M. Bois-le-Duc, he is not a very enviable person."

"Then you are sorry for him?"

"Pardon me, I am not. I have only one feeling towards him, and that would be wiser to keep to myself. Marie, long ago, at Father Point, I saw it all, though you imagined I was so taken up with my painting and my own affairs. I knew McAllister was wholly unworthy of the respect and affection you and M. Bois-le-Duc lavished on him.

"I knew him better than either of you, his weakness, his indecision; but it was not for me to warn you, how could I? Then, Marie, changes came to all of us. McAllister came into his inheritance; you went to seek your fortune; I to work hard in a merchant's office in Montreal. For four years, I labored there at most uncongenial work, but I managed to scrape enough together to pay for my course of study at the school of one of the best masters in Paris. These years of drudgery in Montreal and Paris were only brightened by one hope—a hope I scarcely dared acknowledge to myself, so vain did it appear."

"Yes," said Marie. "But you have succeeded, and your hope has been realized."

"It has not been realized; it is as far from realization as ever."

"I am astonished to hear you speak in such a way after your brilliant success of yesterday."

"Yes, success is satisfactory, and it is a means to an end in this case. Marie, my dear one, through all those long years of drudgery I heard of you only through M. Bois-le-Duc at rare intervals. But, through all that weary time, I never ceased to think of you, though as one far, far removed from me. Then you rose to fame and wealth; to me, a poor struggling artist, further off than ever, and for a time I despaired. You were fêted by the highest in the land, all London was at your feet—what had I to do with the brilliant prima donna? What claim had I to remind her of the old days at Father Point, of my life-long devotion? Oh! Marie, my darling, to keep silence, to think that I might lose you after all, was almost unendurable. Now, though, I *can* speak. I, too, have achieved success as the world counts it. We may now, on that score, meet as equals. Were it not so, I should keep silence always. Marie, I have loved you ever since I knew you. I have watched with interest your whole career, your failures, your successes. I dare not hope my affection is returned—that is too much—and I must ask pardon for having spoken to you today."

The self-possessed prima donna had been very still while Lacroix spoke, and sat shading her face with one hand, and, strange to say, endeavoring to hide the tears which would come in spite of her efforts.

"Marie, speak, my dear one. Have I distressed you? Oh! Marie, I should not have spoken, only the thought of putting the Atlantic between us without telling you was too hard, Marie."

"Eugène, why should you put the Atlantic between us?" said Marie, and something in the expression of her face gave him courage to ask—

"Marie, I am going to Father Point next month. Will you come with me?"

"Yes, Eugène, with you anywhere," placing her hands in his, a look of perfect rest and peace coming over her sweet, care-worn face.

"Remember, Marie," he said gravely, "it is no small thing I ask—to give up your place at the opera, to sacrifice the applause of the world and the pleasing excitement of your life."

"I am tired of it all, Eugène, it is such an empty life."

"And I may be in Canada a whole year—think of it, a year away from London. You must consider all this, and, my dear one, I am not a rich man."

"But I am rich," she said laughing, "very rich, and I never was so glad of it before. Now, have you any more objections to make, for I am beginning to think you don't want me to go to Father Point with you after all."

That night at the opera Mademoiselle Laurentia, the critics said, surpassed herself, though, strange occurrence for usually one so punctual, she kept the audience waiting for a quarter of an hour. Never before had she sung so well.

Great was the indignation of Monsieur Scherzo, her manager, when next day she told him that after this month she would sing no more in public. He swore, he stormed, he tore his hair, and finding threats were in vain he wept in his excitable fashion, but neither threats nor entreaties moved mademoiselle from her decision. "Bah!" he said, "it is the way with them all, a woman can never be a true artist. Directly she rises to any height she goes off and gets married, ten to one to some idiot, who interferes in all her arrangements, and so her career is spoiled. I did think Mademoiselle Laurentia was above such frivolity. I imagined that, at last, I had discovered a true artist, one to whom her art was everything. No, I am again mistaken, and Mademoiselle Laurentia—why, she is not even going to marry a duke, there might be some sense in that, but only a beggarly artist. Bah! what folly!"

Some six weeks later, one sunny afternoon, there came up the Gulf of St. Lawrence a ship crowded with passengers bound for all quarters of the great Dominion. It had been a backward season, and even so late as the beginning of July great icebergs were still floating down the Gulf, huge, white and glistening in the summer sun, as they floated on to their destruction in the southern seas. However, the good ship "Vancouver" passed safely through the perils of storms and icebergs, and after a fairly prosperous passage of ten days arrived safely at Rimouski. There she paused for a few hours to let off the mails and two passengers.

These two passengers had been the cause of a great deal of gossip and attention on the voyage out, for they were both, in their different spheres, celebrated personages, and known to fame on both sides of the Atlantic. It seemed rather strange that they should land at a little out-of-the-way place like Rimouski.

"Oh!" exclaimed one of the celebrities, a little lady clad in furs. "Oh, Eugène, everything is just the same as it used to be in the old days, and look over there on the pier is M. Bois-le-Duc."

Yes, there stood the tall, venerable priest, his hair now snowy white, and his shoulders bent under the weight of years. But the good curé was energetic as of old, and his eyes gleamed with excitement as the ship approached. His hands were stretched out in welcome, and a smile of most intense happiness lighted up his handsome features, and, as the travellers stepped from the gang-way to the pier, he went quickly forward to greet them, exclaiming, in his bright cheery manner:—

"Eugène, Marie, my children, welcome home, a thousand times welcome. Heaven has indeed been good to me. My heart's desire is now fulfilled."

EPILOGUE.

"Our acts our angels are, or good or ill,
The fatal shadows that walk by us still."

Beaumont.

Far up on the east coast of Scotland, where the huge breakers of the Atlantic dash in angry tumult against the granite crags of that rugged shore, stands the castle of Dunmorton, a grim historic pile.

For generations it has been the home of the McAllisters, and is still little changed since the days of Bruce and Balliol, when armed men issued from the low, arched doorway, to work destruction on their enemies of the South.

The last of the race dwells there now; a man yet in the prime of life, though one who takes but little interest in the doings of the busy world. He leads a melancholy and purposeless existence, and seems, as the years go on, to grow more morbid. Some say that he never got over the shock of his wife's sudden death, and that the terrible accident completely shattered his nerves. Others, chiefly, old wives, who have lived on the estate for years, and are deeply versed in all matters connected with their chief's family, shake their heads wisely, and mutter that there is a curse overhanging this branch of the clan. They say it has been so since the '45, when The McAllister of that day turned his son Ivan adrift.

Be that as it may, the present chief is a most miserable man. He has wealth, and everything wealth can command. He has broad lands, power, unbounded influence, for fortune has marked him for one of her favorites. But in the long winter evenings, when the great hall of Dunmorton, with its splendid trophies of the chase and grand oak panelling, is lighted up by the fitful glow of the huge pinewood fire, Noël McAllister sees a vision, which freezes the blood within his veins.

From a dim eerie in the great hall there glides with a slow, noiseless movement a tall, slight lady, clad in a gown of pale green silk. Her snow-white hair is crowned by a cap of finest lace. Her hands are clasped together convulsively, and she stretches them out and sobs in agonized entreaty:

"Oh, Ivan, me bairn! me bonnie bairn, it is sair and lonely wi'out ye here. Will ye no stay wi' us a while longer? Oh! Ivan, me bairn!"

And night after night, so surely as the waves beat against the rocky crag of Dunmorton does the tall pale lady come, always as the clock strikes twelve, no matter who the guests may be. Doors may be barred, every precaution taken, nothing can prevent her entrance.

It comes to pass that after a time gay visitors from London decline The McAllister's invitations, even the splendid shooting of the Glen does not compensate them for the shock to their nerves caused by The McAllister spectre, as they call it. Noël is left much alone, but he has Dunmorton, its broad lands and vast revenues. For these he bartered his honor, his integrity. By his own rule he should be happy, for all his early ambitions are fulfilled. But in truth he has very little happiness or real satisfaction in his prosperity, and there are few even of his poorest neighbors who would care to change places with the "haunted laird."

Far away across the sea, removed from the din and bustle of their busy London lives, for two months in every year, Marie and Eugène Lacroix make their home at Father Point. Although the famous prima donna has retired from public life, still, on the occasion of pilgrimages in honor of the Good St. Anne, she graciously consents to sing for her own people during the celebration of Grand Mass at the pilots' church. There may be heard the clear, sweet notes of the favorite pupil of the good curé, who, after a life spent in good works, has passed to his eternal reward, but the memory of whose sainted example will ever remain in the minds of two people, who owe so much to the holy precepts of Réné Bois-le-Duc, curé of Father Point.

THE END

www.ingramcontent.com/pod-product-compliance
Lightning Source LLC
Chambersburg PA
CBHW020642130626
46552CB00003B/1355